Groundwood Books is grateful for the opportunity to share stories and make books on the Traditional Territory of many Nations, including the Anishinabeg, the Wendat and the Haudenosaunee. It is also the Treaty Lands of the Mississaugas of the Credit. In partnership with Indigenous writers, illustrators, editors and translators, we commit to publishing stories that reflect the experiences of Indigenous Peoples. For more about our work and values, visit us at groundwoodbooks.com.

say yes
and
keep
smiling

Published in English in Canada and the USA in 2023 by Groundwood Books
Translation copyright © 2023 by Shelley Tanaka
Original title: *Rentrer son ventre et sourire, la suite*
Originally published in French (Canada)
Copyright © by Éditions de la Bagnole, Montreal, Canada, 2021

Groundwood Books / House of Anansi Press
groundwoodbooks.com

We gratefully acknowledge for their financial support of our publishing program the
Canada Council for the Arts, the Ontario Arts Council and the Government of Canada.

ONTARIO ARTS COUNCIL
CONSEIL DES ARTS DE L'ONTARIO
an Ontario government agency
un organisme du gouvernement de l'Ontario

Canada Council   Conseil des Arts
for the Arts   du Canada

With the participation of the Government of Canada
Avec la participation du gouvernement du Canada | Canadä

Library and Archives Canada Cataloguing in Publication
Title: Say yes and keep smiling / written by Laurence Beaudoin-Masse ;
translated by Shelley Tanaka.
Other titles: Rentrer son ventre et sourire. Volume 2. English
Names: Beaudoin-Masse, Laurence, author. | Tanaka, Shelley, translator.
Description: Translation of: Rentrer son ventre et sourire. Volume 2.
Identifiers: Canadiana (print) 20220492131 | Canadiana (ebook) 20220492263 |
ISBN 9781773069685 (softcover) | ISBN 9781773069692 (EPUB)
Classification: LCC PS8603.E33678 R4613 2023 | DDC jC843/.6—dc23

Cover art by Clémence Beaudoin
Design by Clémence Beaudoin and Lucia Kim
Printed and bound in Canada

Groundwood Books is a Global Certified Accessible™ (GCA by Benetech) publisher.
An ebook version of this book that meets stringent accessibility standards is available to
students and readers with print disabilities.

Groundwood Books is committed to protecting our natural environment. This book is
made of material from well-managed FSC®-certified forests, recycled materials and other
controlled sources.

MIX
Paper from
responsible sources
FSC® C016245

say yes
and
keep
smiling

WRITTEN BY
Laurence
Beaudoin-Masse

TRANSLATED BY SHELLEY TANAKA

Groundwood Books
House of Anansi Press
Toronto / Berkeley

*"In order for me to meet my goal,
I'm limiting myself to no bread,
no carbs, no sugar, no dairy,
no meat, no fish, no alcohol...
And I'm hungry."*
—Beyoncé, *Homecoming*

INSTAGOOD

Being yourself may be a cute idea in theory, but in practice it's a whole other story. In practice, it takes courage — the courage to disappoint. And I can't bear to do that.

So I adapt. I change. Bit by bit, I perfect and edit myself to show only what I want to show.

Because the idea of not being able to make everyone happy is just too hard. I mean, I try to please everyone. Being agreeable, that's my dream. To not ruffle any feathers.

When I was a teenager, I would have given anything to just stop being me, to start over from scratch. To fit in. I was tired of being invisible, of being such a disappointment. I would have switched places with anyone.

The worst thing is that I succeeded. And everyone loved the new, transformed me. Instead of Élisabeth, I became Ellie. I now have hundreds of thousands of followers on Instagram. I'm one of the top ten most followed YouTubers in Quebec. I've made it, and I'm not the one saying it.

It's just that it's not as much fun as I thought it would be — being a success, I mean.

I often wonder, would anyone love me again if I went back to being just me, without trying to embellish the truth? Or maybe the real question is, could I live without it — without the love of my fans, without their approval? Could I be brave enough to disappoint them?

I used to think so. Everything was so clear. I'd decided to go for it, to listen to myself. I wanted to be myself. I'd got lost along the way and I was going to find myself again. The feeling was so strong, I told myself that wanting it would be enough.

But I had no idea what that actually meant. And I was about to find out.

1

My prefrontal cortex is still buried in a thick fog when Sam stops the live broadcast of his surprise marriage proposal. He lets go of my hand, stands up, removes his phone from the selfie stick and then dives into his phone screen, scrolling through the comments, checking the stats. He's completely preoccupied.

I come to my senses.

"How many people just watched that?" I ask.

"Live? About 6,000, but don't worry. It'll go viral in the next few hours."

There's silence. I'm engaged. I've just received a marriage proposal in front of thousands of people.

In the moment it was intense with the adrenaline and everything, but now...no. The camera's off and I tell myself it all comes down to this. Even in front of thousands of people, in the end it's just the two of us.

I rewind and run through the events in my head. Yesterday, Sam came back from touring with his band. When he arrived, he was cold, distant. Disappointed with how things had gone here while he was away. He thought I was letting myself go, that I was changing.

And then, bam, this morning he asks me to marry him?

What?

Let's just say I wasn't all there. My head had been miles away lately and, oh, by the way, I'd just spent the night with someone else.

Shit! What was I thinking?

I look down at my ring finger, and it's sporting a kind of growth of white gold set with stones and a huge blue diamond. The ring is magnificent, absolutely gorgeous.

I should be happy. I've imagined this moment so often, imagined that it would be one of the most beautiful days of my life. I refuse to believe that I've just blown it.

In a panic, I try to pump myself up, look happy. And I wait, hoping for the feeling to come. But the silence, the banality of those seconds ticking away is almost unbearable.

Sam finally lifts his eyes from his screen and looks at me happily.

"You're happy, aren't you?"

"Of course. Absolutely."

Ten minutes ago, I was sneaking in after spending

the night with Dave. I came back hoping that my face wouldn't show that I'd just cheated on my boyfriend. My God, that sounds so dramatic — cheating. I've never done that in my life, not even close. I am basically an infidelity amateur. An adultery newbie.

When I got home, I was sure Sam would suspect something. That he'd be worried. That I'd have to reassure him by being super relaxed, easygoing and normal. Make up a few casual details about spending the evening with my sister. Hide the truth a bit to give myself time to decide what to do — about us.

And then just like that, we're engaged. To Be Married.

My feet weigh six hundred pounds. My head is floating like a party balloon.

"I'm going to take a bath," I say. "I stink. It always smells like stale smoke at Alice's, you know?"

And so it begins. The first lie of the day. Okay, the second. I did tell Sam I was "happy." Not to mention saying, "Yes, I will." Maybe that was a lie, too...

I don't know. I don't know anymore. I know nothing.

Okay, so let's say that's two and a half lies today.

And it's not even 9:00 a.m.

Things are starting out well.

Top 10 YouTubers
CAN/FR

1. Jordanne Jacques – 807,000 followers
2. Tellement Cloé – 764,000 followers
3. Cath Bonenfant – 505,000 followers
4. **Ellie – Quinoa Forever – 503,000 followers**
5. Mila Mongeau – 501,000 followers
6. Emma & Juju – 449,000 followers
7. Approved by Gwen – 428,000 followers
8. Sophie Chen – 344,000 followers
9. Maëla Djeb – 162,000 followers
10. Zoé around the World – 145,000 followers

I rush to the bathroom and close the door. Breathe in. Breathe out. I look at myself in the mirror. Not impressed. I run my hand over my face to try to erase the evidence — the lack of sleep, the doubts, the lies.

Sigh. I take off my ring, suddenly freeze. I'm holding several thousand dollars between my thumb and index finger. What should I do with this? I tear off a long piece of toilet paper and fold it into a little cushion and put it on the edge of the sink.

I'll put the ring on that. There.

I take off my jeans, my panties, my socks. I sit on the toilet, push my clothes away with my feet.

Think. I have to think. But I'm too nervous. I can see the ring out of the corner of my eye. It sparkles. I get the feeling it's mocking me. I stare at it. It stares back. It sparkles some more.

Did it move? I hold my breath. I am suddenly very afraid that it's going to fall down the drain if I breathe on it too hard. I get up, pick it up carefully, and finally decide to put it in the medicine cabinet on top of a giant bottle of ibuprofen.

Okay. It'll be safe there.

I start to breathe again. I wonder how I'm going to take care of it every day. It feels like at least as much responsibility as owning a small pet.

I have a pee, then I turn on the taps and fill the tub as high as it will go. I check the temperature with my finger. It's boiling. I add more hot, I want it to be burning hot. I want to wash away all the doubts, sterilize my soul. Then while I'm at it, I add lots of lavender bath gel to anesthetize my nervous system. Excellent.

I finish undressing, pull my fleece over my head. It smells like Dave. I breathe in deeply. It reminds me of his eyes on me, his hands on me.

No, no, no. Don't go there. Need to focus.

I'm undoing my bra when Sam knocks on the door. I drop the bra on the floor, grab my sweater that stinks of guilt, roll it up into a ball, toss it in the cupboard under the sink and throw myself into the tub like I'm Bruce Willis in *Die Hard*.

I tell Sam he can come in. He opens the door, pokes his head around it and says I've just received two big parcels.

And then he stays there, like he's searching for words.

It's not like him…

He gives himself a little shake and says, "I was wondering…"

"Yeah?"

"Are you going to post?"

"About?"

"The ring. To show it off. People are asking about it a lot in the comments. They want to see it."

"Oh…I don't know. I guess I could."

"Okay!" He looks like he wants to say something else, but hesitates.

I frown at him.

"What?"

"If you could just tag Maison Perks in your post."

"…Okay."

"Cool."

"Yeah. Cool."

"I love you…"

"Mmmm-hmmm. Me, too."

Sam closes the door. It hits me. I get it.

But of course. What did I expect? I dunk my head

under the scalding water. My brain is turning into a hard-boiled egg.

My ring is sponsored. The marriage proposal is sponsored.

I don't know whether I feel consoled or enraged.

SPONSORED

The first time I got a partnership — a real one — I was sure I was going to get called out. That I'd be criticized for selling out, being self-serving. That it wouldn't be acceptable. I was already used to getting free products and special invitations, but this time I was being paid. It was an amount that seems ridiculously low today — but at the time I was super happy, even honored. Two hundred dollars for including @alohacoco water in one of my photos. I wasn't that familiar with the product, but even if I wasn't that convinced by the taste, I ended up getting used to it. I prepared my post, clicked Share and waited for the first reactions with my heart pounding and my belly churning.

And then... nothing. People clicked Like and that was that. Meh.

Even today, no one cares about content placement in my posts. Partnerships have even become a sign of success, of privileged status. Now there are two kinds of users on the networks — ordinary people and us professionals. While everyone is there to share their thing or exchange their news, we come with our professional cameras, our skills, our war machine in full view. We take in the love and the love money. And everyone thinks it's all...just great.

On one condition, that is. You have to "stay true." You have the right to promote products as long as you stay real, remain honest, are a good person. Authenticity is the unwritten law of the web, the content creator's code of conduct.

And everyone insists on it, including me.

But when you think about it, it's still amazing how much importance we attach to the integrity of people we don't even know. People who earn their living selling their image, selling the good life. What difference does it make whether it's true or not?

No, but I get it! I follow people, too. I get attached to human beings living in Boisbriand, Seattle, Paris, Los Angeles. I have a friend who loves light red wines, erotic literature and seashells, but who knows nothing at all about me. Another friend who can make soups to die for that I will never even taste. I love these people. I'm being sincere when I comment with heart eyes emojis on photos of their newborns. I'm touched when they say they hope I'm well, always using the same tone and phrasing. Ecstatic when they FINALLY show me around their apartments. I'm interested when they decide to open up, be vulnerable, when they cry in black and white. Comforted that they're just human beings with a few jump cuts added. I'm moved, too, when I see that golden light beaming on their kitchen #goldenhour.

My emotions are real, and I hope the show is, too. I believe it. So what if they're talking to me about shampoo, underwear, ready-to-eat meals. I like, so I buy.

Tell me everything. Tell me the story, the one with the happy ending. Tell it to me again, please.

I subscribe to personalities who, in exchange for one-sided intimacy and a bit of a dream, include the #ad in their content because they have to make a living. That goes without saying. Right, it goes without saying... that by clicking Like we're voting for people who we hope are sufficiently "authentic" to represent the face of mass consumption. To represent it kindly, as a way of saying, "I hope you're doing well." They may be our advertising friends, but they are still friends, nonetheless.

It's great. I also hope you are well. I also have something to sell. It's perfect...

No, I'm not complaining. It's just that I always

thought I was in control, that I was the one pulling the strings, that I was the one doing the influencing. But it's funny. I don't know anymore if I'm the one who's doing the advertising, or the one who is being advertised.

CELEBRITY WORLD

We love Samuel Vanasse's surprise marriage proposal to Ellie of Quinoa Forever!

Samuel Vanasse and Élisabeth Bourdon-Marois have officially upgraded their relationship status to "Engaged"! The handsome singer took his sweetheart by surprise by asking for her hand live on her YouTube channel. Hello, romance! We still have the chills from seeing so much love flowing between these two . . .

Samantha Larochelle denounces violent and fatphobic comment

Samantha Larochelle, who uses social media in a super positive way, received an extremely malicious comment this week that has upset her, with good reason! The influencer, singer, actress and author did not want to conceal the harassment of which she was the victim, which is why she has shared the message in question. Warning, the content of this one is extremely shocking . . .

10 personalities who had the courage to expose the sexual harassment they have experienced

The wave of denunciations that has been sweeping social

media since the beginning of the fall has resulted in several courageous people coming forward to condemn the sexual harassment they have suffered. Among the hundreds of testimonials, a few public figures have spoken up to tell their own stories . . .

3

When I leave the bathroom, I stumble over the two large cardboard boxes that have just been delivered.

I look at the shipping labels. They're from my publisher.

My book is here! I'm so thrilled. I'm finally going to be able to hold it in my hands. MY BOOK. I've worked so hard for this.

I can't wait, even in a towel, with wet feet. I run to get a knife and cut through the thin layer of adhesive tape on one of the boxes. Inside, I find twenty copies featuring my smiling face on the cover.

I'm leaning against the island in a kitchen flooded with light, holding a basket of fresh produce — kale, raspberries, lemons, a watermelon. My smile is dazzling, my teeth are whiter than white. My hair ripples over my shoulders. I'm wearing a leaf-green dress fitted at the waist. My face is slim, my stomach is flat, my arms are tiny.

I am magnificent.

I stand there in the hallway staring at my image. Hypnotized. I . . . okay, I've put on some weight since the photos were taken — a few pounds — but I can't believe I used to be that person. I didn't realize I was perfect. I've seen the photo before, but seeing it for real on the book with the title, the glossy cover stock, it is just...awesome.

I flip through the pages. Ellie cooking. Motivational phrases. Ellie stretching. Grocery lists. Plates brimming with vitamins. Ellie eating with gusto.

I love her, this girl. I just love her. The recipes, the routines. She makes me want to drink my plant-based milk, make gluten-free muffins for my neighbors, drink a herbal tea. She makes me want to live well. It's inspiring.

I close the book. My eyes look down at my toes. They're a little crooked. Peeling polish. Have to fix that. Have to fix...what, exactly? My toes. What?

I'm standing here in the hall staring at my feet. The pale gray of the walls, the soft light. I feel a heaviness in my chest, as if someone is pushing on it with the palm of their hand.

My book launch is in twenty-two days. I tell myself...twenty-two days.

I have twenty-two days to become that girl again.

#SCROLLING

– It's the season for cozy sweaters! @cotn

– This man! When I'm with you @marc_cut I'm always in my element.

– Find inspiration in nature @purejoymakeup

– BELIEVE IN YOURSELF

– You can find me here all weekend soaking up the sun and drinking wine thanks to @hotelduquai

– It's been 2 months since I started taking medication to help my mental health.

– Self-care essentials: wine, eye cream and lemons!

– It's true that it can be super scary switching to a 100% natural deodorant like @flowerpower!

– Last year I had no choice but to cut down a magnificent oak on my property. I cried that day.

– What motivates me to be here: to share my passion for wellness and drop a nice big smile into your feed! At GO, we smile. GO!

– Therapy was tough today.

– BTW, I'm wearing an outfit from my favorite brand @BananaApparel

– About to eat LOTS of spaghetti.

– Don't be fooled, this pic was taken in the morning before eating!

– What I'm about to say might sound weird, but I inspire myself. I look at my favorite pictures of myself, and it motivates me to get back to the gym!

– Save water, drink champagne.

– Classic morning for me except my hair usually looks way worse.

– People often ask me for relationship advice, and I would probably say wait and find the right one, don't wait for them to turn into the right one.

– Loungewear is great, but try your jeans on once in a while, it's the best way to avoid #bingeeating

– I FEEL GOOD!!!

– We must stop comparing ourselves to others.

– My Booty Program is FINALLY available.

– Use code MILA20 for 20% off on your purchase @seacollagen

– Fall is my favorite season and I plan to make the most of it.

– Give a thumbs up if you're a runner, too!

– Curves are beautiful. @bellaKingston is my #bodygoal

– Give yourself a hug today.

– Here are my 5 tips for staying motivated.

– A little pick-me-up in my cute new mugs from @XYHome

– Chase the light to combat seasonal depression.

– The next time you feel like giving up exercise, tell yourself: I WILL CONTINUE TO DO IT FOR ME

– Your Mondays don't have to be boring!

– A little reminder that I am human just like everyone else. I choose the photos that show off my best features.

– My underwear is so comfy, I thought I was taking nudes

– What good things are you up to these days?

4

Mother-daughter yoga, middle row. Alexandra invites us to set an intention for the rest of the day and place it in our hearts. Mine is...to...I'm going to...concentrate...it's to...ah, right.

To know what I fucking want.

Hey, that's how it comes to me. I'm not going to censor my deep intuition on account of swear words, right? I concentrate super hard.

To know what I fucking want.

Dave-Sam-Dave-Sam?

Ommmmm.

My mother is considerably less animated than usual. No comments every two seconds, no sexy outfit, no urgent questions about the alignment of her pelvis.

In short, it's like a breath of fresh air.

Ever since my mother and Nico officially became a couple, they decided that it would be better for her to take Alexandra's classes. It would seem that my mother radiates a sexual energy that upsets Nico's chakras and makes it hard for him to properly teach his yoga classes.

It would also seem this is way too much information. God help me.

"Eka pada rajakapotasana," Alexandra says. "King Pigeon pose."

King Pigeon. Right. Majestic Rat, Sympathetic Hyena, Gracious Cow. How many other ridiculous and impossible personality traits will yoga impose on the animal kingdom?

Oops. Did I say that out loud? Because my mother is giving me a Look. I shake my head to tell her to forget it. Great, now I've lost my intention. To know. Breathe in. To know. Breathe out. To know. I hold my breath...I picture Dave's eyes. His hands. Aghh!

To be honest, I've wanted to message him three hundred and fifty times since the day before yesterday. To tell him I had a nice evening, that I think about him all the time. That I'm engaged — LOL — but maybe not...?

What isn't clear is whether that would bother him. I've abandoned the plan three hundred and fifty times. I know how these things work. Must wait at least three or four days to see who cracks first. It's a mind game. He'll message me.

I have to be patient, I can do it.

Can I do it?

∞

After class, my mother insists that we go for a walk in the park across from the studio. This is a first. I'm suspicious. Something's up.

For the hundredth time she says she's ecstatic about Sam's "bold" marriage proposal. Tells me about her new technique for preparing green lentils. Asks me yet again whether we've chosen a weekend for the wedding. Or even a season, at least? I dodge her questions as best I can, but it's difficult. I wonder whether she suspects something. If that's why we're here.

I'm about to invent an excuse to casually flee the scene when she finally gets to the reason behind our epic stroll.

"Okay, so I wanted to let you know that Nico and I are going on vacation tomorrow for three weeks... no plans or schedule, just us and our backpacks!"

"Your backpacks."

"Yes, to Mexico. I'll be back in time for your book launch."

"Oh. Okay, cool! I'm happy for you!"

I may look excited, but the truth is that I still don't know what to think about her relationship with Nico. With their twenty-one-year age difference.

I would like to be happy for her, but…I just hope she's not paying for his plane ticket. That she's not using her retirement savings to finance trips for a guy in his twenties. A backpacking trip…doesn't sound like something you'd do with your fifty-year-old girlfriend. I accept that traveling is formative when you're young, but it's not the fountain of youth.

Still, I force myself to be nice.

"Is this why you wanted to go for a 'chat in the park'? Because I want you to know, Maman, that you don't have tiptoe around me every time you make plans with Nico. That's entirely your bus —"

"I know, but no, it's your father, Ellie. I want you to check on him. His cancer, it's not looking good… it's…I talked to him on the phone…things are bad."

I stop walking. I look at my mother, wait for her to say something, to explain, but grief suddenly catches us off guard. It's too much…

She looks away as I try to process this information.

"What do you mean by bad?" I ask.

"You need to call him…phone him."

"Okay."

"I can't…I can't cope with it. I…no."

33

"..."

"I just can't."

She stares at the horizon. Avoids my gaze. My feelings have always been too much for her.

PAPA

My father grew up in the woods. In the last village before the road turns into gravel. He moved to Montreal when he was about ten, when his parents separated. Divorce was rare back then. Let's just say things weren't easy with his father. He never really wanted to talk to me about it, and I never asked him questions about it, either. I think he was a messed-up person, my grandfather. I think he messed up a lot of other people, too.

As an adult, my father still loved the forest and big open spaces. He was a kind of a professorial adventurer-fisherman. He bought our cottage just before I was born — a tiny house by the river surrounded by a forest of maple and pine. Just for us, to raise hares, hunt, collect syrup. A place to look after and protect.

When I was little, I spent every summer there. Sometimes my father took me to sleep under the stars. In the forest, by the shore. His favorite hunting spot. A rocky plateau on the edge of the water. Just me and him with marshmallows and our sleeping bags. He'd light a big fire that would burn all night long. I'd try to spot bats in the night sky. I listened to the tide rise and fall.

I liked that. The huge vault of sky. The endless stars. Me no bigger than a pebble. Just a tiny bit of fly poop in the universe.

It was sweet, it was everything. I felt good there, and he did, too, I think.

He did, too.

5

This morning I'm shooting new videos with Mila at home. We start with a Try-On Haul.

The concept is simple. We were contacted by Style Republic, who let us choose five hundred dollars' worth of clothes from their site. We try them on and give our impressions on the style, price and quality.

Mila sets up the lights while I wrestle with my mascara. I have a big pack of eyelashes that are all stuck together. The more I try to separate them, the worse it gets. I keep at it, hoping for a miracle. Big mistake. Right now I'm wearing a mono eyelash. It sucks.

The other thing that sucks is that the collaboration between Mila and me is working well. Too well. We've decided to release a video every two weeks until spring. So now we're a bit stuck with continuing to be "friends," even though I am officially on high alert — ever since we filmed that project for Beyond Swimwear. It's impossible that she just happened to forget to warn me that I would have to wear a tiny bikini during the interview. Impossible. I fell into that trap like a rank amateur.

I just don't understand why she did it, but

whatever. I'm on my guard now, so nothing can happen, right?

Mila sits down on my bed.

"You're getting married! I can't believe it! That's huge."

"I know!"

"Have you started making plans?"

"Well...I'm cleaning up my Pinterest board. Lots of pins to organize, so it's taking a while."

She grabs one of the garment bags filled with new clothes.

"If you're interested, I can help you come up with an aesthetic for the events for your big day. I've got lots of ideas! Have you thought about your color palette yet?"

"Um. Events? What events?"

"Well, the engagement party, the bridesmaid proposal, the —"

I raise my eyebrow. "Bridesmaid what?"

"Proposal...It's like a marriage proposal, except it's for your attendants. You organize a surprise to ask them to be your bridesmaids! You serve a few things to eat — maybe a special cheese platter, theme cookies, champagne — and offer a meaningful gift to show them how much you appreciate them being part of the most important day of your life."

Mila talks quickly, as if she's got some kind of post-doctorate in wedding planning from Harvard.

It's giving me a headache. I haven't even thought about choosing bridesmaids. I'm not sure my sister is going to be thrilled at the thought.

"Then there's the bridal shower, the bachelorette party, the rehearsal dinner. You can also have a welcome party if you want, and there's the morning-after brunch...What else? Oh, yes. The actual WEDDING, ha, ha!"

"I...I haven't really had time to think about it yet, but I'll let you know soon!"

Soon as in Never. She'll probably arrange for me to walk down the aisle wearing a bikini, or worse.

"Anyway, the surprise marriage proposal was brilliant," she says. "We never heard another word about your poutine story after that. Really solid move. Strong."

I'm secretly laughing. She talks with so much confidence, when she has no idea. There is absolutely no connection between my wedding and that photo of me eating poutine that went viral. The photo that everyone and their sister found hilarious, but which almost cost me an important contract and my relationship with Sam.

"Oh, but the timing wasn't deliberate," I tell her. "It just happened like that."

She looks at me like she's wondering if I'm joking.

"Sure," she says. And she winks.

Oh my God, why didn't I think of this before? I am such an idiot! It's so obvious now. Sam's marriage proposal was a public relations move. A strategy to defuse the controversy.

Arggh. It's worse than I thought. I am more confused now than ever.

I make another little mental tick mark in the column headed "Sam doesn't really love me," and force myself to give Mila a big smile. Make her think I'm in on the game but just can't talk about it.

Folding a pile of clothes to try on, she says, "And you must be happy that you have FINALLY moved ahead of me. You've got more followers than me now."

"Oh, well, maybe. I don't know..."

I have two thousand more than she does. I count. Regularly.

"Anyway," she says, "it doesn't bother me. My engagement rate has been super good lately, and my TikTok has really taken off."

"That's great."

"Sam's done a lot for you, hasn't he? It's hot. My God, what would you do without him?"

"Lots of things! I...I'd manage."

"I'm really happy for you!"

Happy my ass. Mila is one of the most ambitious people I know. It's impossible that she is "happy" that my ratings are higher than hers. I'm positive she is not indifferent to the fact that it's me — the girl who was always less cool than her, the girl who ruined her big art project at the end of high school — who is now more successful than she is. She's already planning her next move, for sure. But in the meantime, I can savor my victory.

And just so that she doesn't assume I'm as naive as she thinks, I add, "You would have every right to not be happy. As you often say, there's no need for us to pretend to be friends."

"True. But it doesn't mean we're not a team. I've got your back, Ellie, don't forget it!"

It's funny. I don't believe her for two seconds.

"But if you have my back, as you say, why didn't you warn me that I'd have to wear a bikini to take part in that project with Jordanne? It's not like it was some minor detail. I was super uncomfortable, and I got the impression you were setting me up."

She looks surprised. I am, too. I never would have thought I'd dare say what I was thinking.

I can see her weighing her words before she replies.

"OMG, no, never! I didn't think you'd mind showing your body the way it is."

"But I'd already told you that I didn't feel super confident about my body. You knew that it...wasn't easy for me."

"Yeah, but you were also saying how we shouldn't reinforce stereotypes and blah, blah, blah."

"Okay, but what difference does that make?"

"Well, I think you should celebrate your body, Ellie. It's important to learn to love yourself the way you are, perfectly imperfect!"

This is the kind of talk that makes me want to scream into my pillow.

"Besides," she says, "don't worry. The interview was awesome! Super moving, and I'm sure it helped lots of other people love themselves, too. It was a nice touch. Jordanne was really happy. No kidding, you should do it more often. It's a great niche for you, self-love. Like Sarah Coutu and her photos that show her cellulite, you know what I'm talking about? There are lots of brands that love that. Not all of them, but a lot!"

She smiles, showing off her tiny, perfectly straight white teeth, winks at me and says, "No hard feelings?"

I just don't believe this. I clench my jaw.

"Of course," I say. "No hard feelings."

Game on, Mila. Game on.

6

I focus my energy and concentrate my gaze, tilting my head a bit to find the best angle.

First, smile with your eyes. I stare at the camera, relax my mouth, let a bit of air flow between my lips. Sam stands behind the kitchen island, takes the photos quickly without talking. I gently wave the bouquet of parsley in my hands. Change the position of my chin. Higher, lower. More smiley. More serious. I've done this thousands of times, but each time means starting again. Taking successful photos always means starting from scratch.

I breathe in, smile with my eyes. Breathe in, smile with my eyes. Breathe...

Sam stops photographing, hands me the device. I'm hyperventilating. I'm full of hope as I check out the images. I scroll through at least a hundred.

I don't like them. I feel ugly.

"Can we just take a few more?" I say. "I'm going to try something else. It's not there yet."

I give him back the camera and pick up the parsley. I know we've been working on the same photo for half an hour already, but it's got to have the right look. Be up to the standard of the images in the book. There is no other option.

Sam is in the middle of answering a message on his phone.

"Come on, Ellie," he says distractedly. "The photos are good. I can't do better than that."

I understand the implication. He doesn't think he can do better because I'm not pretty enough. Because I've gained weight.

I pick off little bits of parsley and flick them to the ground.

"Would you have asked me to marry you if I weighed ten, twenty...or whatever pounds more? At what point would you stop loving me?"

"What?"

He's surprised. He thinks I'm joking.

But I'm serious.

"The other night, before the Karma Christmas dinner, in the bedroom, remember? You said you thought I was letting myself go, that you were afraid I was going back to 'the way I was before.' That I was putting the weight back on that I'd lost. I can read between the lines. You think I'm ugly now."

He realizes what we're talking about, that I haven't

just moved on to other things since his marriage proposal.

He covers his face with his hands and lets them drop to his sides.

"Are you kidding me?" he says, looking annoyed.

"Hey, stop it, okay? I have a right to be angry. I have a right to —"

"Sure, yeah, you have a right, except all I said was that I was scared. I did not say I didn't think you were beautiful or that I didn't want to be with you...Stop taking everything I say and twisting it. You always do that!"

Irritated, I put up my hand to make him stop talking.

"You know what? Just drop it. I'll sort it out without you."

That makes him smile. He comes over to me and says, all sweetness, "Ellie, it's a beautiful day, can you not make a big deal out of it? Besides, you are super beautiful."

"Yeah, that's just it..."

"You are the most gorgeous."

"Ah, please, just...stop it."

I roll my eyes. Smile in spite of my anger, quickly

hide my face so he doesn't think I'm happy.

It has been haunting me for three days. Thinking about how disappointed and worried he was. How much he thinks I've changed. I resent him for that... I blame myself for that. Just hearing him call me beautiful makes me feel relieved. Very.

"It's just that..." he adds.

"What?"

"It's just that I don't know her, the girl you used to be... It's true that I'm worried that you're changing. It's not a crime. You've put on a few pounds... that's all."

I don't feel relieved after all. I just wish he would say the right thing. That he would give me a good reason to forget about it.

Instead he says, "It's hypothetical, okay? We're just talking here."

He slips one hand around my waist, strokes my hair with the other.

"Right," I say. "We're just talking."

"You get involved with someone, you choose this person above *all* the others because you love her exactly the way she is... you marry her, then two or three years later, you find yourself with a completely different person! Put yourself in my place. If that happened, and I say *if*, it would be disappointing, admit it!"

I stare down at the bunch of parsley in my hand. Poor little parsley looks at least as unhappy as I feel right now.

"Be honest now," Sam says. "Would you love me the same if I stopped working out? If I stopped my music? If my face were different?"

"Well…"

"See!"

"Yes, no, but. If I did happen to put on weight, I would still be me! I wouldn't be someone else, another person. I would be me. I am me! I am always me no matter what."

My voice has suddenly started to get way too high. I'm on the verge of tears, and I pray that he'll say the thing that will change everything. That will make everything okay.

But instead…

"Ellie, I'm sorry, but there isn't a guy around who doesn't want his girlfriend to be hot. That's the way it is. Anyone who says otherwise is a hypocrite."

I sigh loudly.

"Maybe. But I could be beautiful with a different body!"

"Yes."

"Good! Thank you!"

My shoulders relax a bit.

"You just wouldn't be my type," he adds.

PRETTY GIRLS

I always wanted to be beautiful. For me it was clear — get pretty or die trying. When I was little, I would stand in front of the mirror for a long time, examining myself carefully. I wanted to know. Was I beautiful or not? I understood that my body was important. I examined the look in my eyes, the way I moved my lips, evaluated myself from every angle.

But no matter how long I spent, I was never sure. So I would try to catch myself off guard. I'd shoot a quick glance at the mirror at an unexpected moment. To see myself before I recognized myself. Like I would look at a stranger. To judge.

Beautiful or not? I wanted to know.

Because no matter what I was going to do in my life, it would be better to do it as a pretty girl.

As a young adult, I did everything, absolutely everything, to make myself beautiful. I didn't want to be beautiful in my own way, I wanted be beautiful period. Beautiful like the fitgirls, happygirls, baby-girls, healthylivinggirls. Girls with full lips looking out at the world with delight. Who travel around the planet in a bathing suit — always a new one. Kneeling in the sand, spending their mornings nibbling on a croissant but never taking a real bite. Reading books that match their outfits. Girls whose glass of rosé is always full. Who wear dresses that never get wrinkled. Who eat spaghetti in their underwear. Who fall madly in love with their turtlenecks. Lounge on the couch half-undressed in the middle of the afternoon. Take baths at all hours of the day. Wrap themselves in fluffy robes that slip off their shoulders. Fulfilled. Girls whose lips part just slightly when they laugh. Who can talk to you about personal growth while wearing a thong in a field of sunflowers. Girls with perfect peach butts making the peace sign. Who have the pleasure of existing while being sleek and beautiful, who seem to want for nothing. Nothing but to be looked at, their arms hanging loosely by their sides as they stare into the camera. Model girls.

All my life I've turned being beautiful into a project, like reaching for the sun. I work at being beautiful, at being an object of desire. I've created a body that is not mine. I try to play the role. It's difficult, and yet — it goes without saying — I fall down, I get up again. Of course. I don't want anything else but to be able to keep going one more time.

So tell me, you fitgirls, happygirls, babygirls, healthylivinggirls — have you found your bliss? Tell me I'll make it one day, that I haven't wasted my time, wasted my joy. That happiness exists and it's always wearing a new bikini, and it has nice round buttocks.

That it's not in vain, that the day will come when I will be beautiful enough.

Finally.

You have sent a message to David Lanctôt

E: So what's new, David Lanctôt? Maybe I'm thinking about you.

E: Often.

E: #justsaying

7

I took my mother's advice and called my father to check on him. I had to tell him about the wedding anyway.

He was happy, and I was relieved. You never know with him. I offered to come around to see him at work. Normally I don't really like spending time with him, but it's different there. We arranged to meet in the university cafeteria for lunch.

I've been waiting for about ten minutes when he walks in. Our eyes meet, and I smile at him as though I don't know about his illness. As if everything is fine. He waves and gestures that he's going to get something to eat. Then I watch him move through the crowd of students. The eminent Jacques Marois. The much-loved professor — admired, praised for the remarkable quality of his teaching. For his "invaluable" contributions.

When I was younger I would often be asked what it was like to be the daughter of a "great man." Tough, I wanted to say. It was tough. But I understood that no one really wanted to know. So I said it was great, and that was enough.

I watch my father consult the daily menu, take a tray. His head high, his shoulders straight and proud. No one would suspect, but I know. I can see it in the small, awkward movements of his hands. I can sense that he is off-balance. That he's scared of disappearing.

The man who had been so big suddenly looks small to me.

So small.

PAPA

When I was little, I often went to the university with my father. I loved going to work with him. I always made sure to leave my childcare coupons for professional development days in my lunch box or at the bottom of my locker. For one whole day, without childcare, my life took a glamorous turn. My father would take me to his office, and I would attend his literature classes while I drew pictures of princess dresses with felt markers or read spooky novels. I felt much more comfortable in a lecture hall in the middle of a hundred adults than at school surrounded by twenty of my classmates.

At the start of each lecture, my father would take the time to introduce me, his eldest daughter. He always joked that he was busy training the next generation and that given that *War and Peace* alone was almost 1,500 pages long, it was good to start young. For a single minute, all eyes were on me. Indulgent, attentive. I would look embarrassed, but the truth was that I loved it. I adored being the center of attention. It was a wonderful feeling, but short-lived, and as soon as it was over, I lived for the next time, my next moment of glory, when all eyes would be on me.

At lunch time, we would eat spaghetti in the cafeteria. Meat sauce for him, tomato sauce for me. With a slice of white bread, margarine and a small mountain of Parmesan. The fake stuff, which was the best. We would wash it down with a nice glass of cold milk. It was one thing my mother never understood, that mix of tomatoes and milk. It always made her cringe. I confess that I didn't understand the appeal, either, but at the time I would do anything to be on the same team as my father. Even if it meant pretending that I liked the same questionable flavor combinations — milk with tomato sauce, mustard with shepherd's pie, jam with grilled cheese or, worst of all, apple juice with cereal.

To be my father's daughter, to be on the same level as my father. It wasn't that I never tried. It was just that I never succeeded.

8

Jacques has been sitting across from me with his tray for the past two minutes. A small soup, daily special, dessert cup, glass of milk. For two minutes I've stopped breathing. My bench makes weird little noises when I move. I don't know what to say. I haven't even dared to ask him how he's doing. The truth is I'm afraid he'll feel he has to tell me the truth, and I won't know what to do with it. Not now. I'm not ready.

"It's good to see you, Papa," I say.

He smiles, unwraps his plastic utensils, takes a mouthful of soup from his Styrofoam bowl. I guess the university didn't get the memo about the imminent demise of life on this planet thanks to single-use plastics.

When he brings the little white spoon to his mouth, I notice that his hand trembles. A lot. Drops of cream of mushroom fall on his shirt. He looks down, sees the damage.

I look away. I don't want him to know that I've noticed. He would see the pity in my eyes.

Anything but that.

I need to say something diverting. Think, Ellie. Think quick.

I rummage through my bag and take out one of my copies of *Radiant*, put on a cheerful face.

"Look! It's my book! Okay, so it's just recipes, exercise routines and little happiness tips...I mean, it's not...great literature or anything...but it's my book. I put a lot of love into it."

My father sticks his hand in his vest and pulls out a cloth handkerchief. He wipes his shirt.

"Thank you, coco-pomme."

Coco-pomme. He used to call me that. I haven't forgotten. How I loved it when he called me that. Coco-pomme.

His eyes meet mine. It feels really funny, I feel a bit numb, but I manage to return his gaze. Look straight into those small blue eyes — eyes I've often found so hard, so cold. The eyes I spent years avoiding now suddenly seem so tender. Defenseless.

I look away. Mumble something or other.

I hear my sister's voice behind me.

"Sorry, sorry, sorry. I'm late. BUT, you love me anyway. Admit it!"

I swallow the strange feeling in my throat while

Alice slides a tray filled with spaghetti, a triple chocolate cookie and a can of orange soda on the table.

"Sorry. I stayed behind to talk to my prof. It seems he doesn't realize that freedom of speech is just an outdated liberal concept that mainly benefits supporters of the status quo. He's exhausting."

Alice kisses my father on the cheek. She gives me a look that turns from playful to exasperated.

"You brought your lunch, Ellie? Really?"

"I had leftovers."

"Girl, this is a cafeteria."

"Exactly."

Without asking permission, Alice opens my high-end lunch box to examine the contents. She looks at each Tupperware like it's filled with space-age food.

My father, meanwhile, decides to leaf through my book. I hold my breath. I want him to say something — something nice, anything…

But Alice speaks first.

"Crudités?"

"Yes, crudités."

"I think the last time I ate celery, I still had training wheels on the back of my bike."

"Too bad for you, because celery is brimming with fiber."

"Ooh, yum. Fiber! I've heard that there's also lots of that in — what is it called...?"

"..."

"Hay."

She opens her can of soda and it makes a big *pssht.* Swallows a mouthful and continues her skewering.

"Okay, then. Raw vegetables, a hard-boiled egg and...an apple. Not even a little bit of dip?"

"You're making fun, Alice Bourdon-Marois. Stop it."

"But you're going to starve to death! Look at this! Is it so you'll fit into your wedding gown?"

"Stop! You're being annoying!"

"No, I'm being *rational.*"

I give my sister the death stare. She's gone far enough. Not in front of my father. In any case, I'm the one who decides what I eat. And I've been on a good food roll for two days. Bitch, don't kill my vibe. I certainly have nothing to learn from a girl who is about to ingest about...60 + 40 + 30...roughly 130 grams of simple carbs. For lunch. On a Wednesday.

"So what's new, Pops? Are you feeling okay? Due for tests soon?"

My father places *Radiant* on the table and picks up his spoon. He stares at his soup, looking for words.

I haven't said anything to Alice about what Maman said after yoga, to watch out for him, that things were looking bad. I know, I know. On a scale of courage, I'm in the nervous duckling category. But I just couldn't do it. Instead I invited myself to their traditional Wednesday meal.

My father takes his time before answering.

"They did the tests... the news isn't what we'd hoped for, girls. The cancer has already spread to several organs — the lungs, among others. In the best-case scenario, the doctors think I have a few months, maybe a bit more."

Alice frowns.

"Before you start treatment?"

My father crumples up his handkerchief.

"There won't be any treatments, dear. It's the end of the road for me."

My sister answers with her mouth full.

"Hey, you're still not going to die!"

And I see that it hits her for the first time. That she realizes. He's going to die. Papa is going to die.

Her eyes fill with water. So do my father's. They

look at each other without being able to speak.
Frozen. Drowning.

As for me, I lower my head. I want to show them
how sad I am. That I'm upset. That it's the end of the
world for me, too.

I try hard. Really hard.

But nothing comes out.

Fuck. Nothing comes out.

9

I came here without second-guessing. I had to come.

I push open the door to Café B, and the wooden floor squeaks as I walk into the small café, which is already full of customers. At the counter, Dave and an employee are filling takeout orders. The line is long and they are hard at it. I see Dave from a distance and my heart melts. I always forget the effect he has on me, how his atoms collide with my own.

I sit at one of the few free tables. I try to hide my nervousness, look normal. I take out a bunch of things from my bag. A notebook, pencils, a packet of gum, my book. I pretend to start to work on... something or other. I tell myself it's a just a matter of time before Dave sees me, too. Before he comes over to talk to me, so happy to see me. That it's like a game we play.

Relax, Ellie. It's a game. Except...

What if he doesn't see me? If he never realizes I'm here? Argh. I'm going to have to go over to him right away, otherwise it will look weird. I'll have to stand in line like everyone else.

Oh, my God, this is awkward.

No. It's impossible. I pretend to be busy with my phone. I open the calendar app and scribble in my notebook. I write down things like "Revise invitations list for *Radiant* launch," "Confirm menu with Jean-Fé," and "January strategy." Things that vaguely make sense.

I try not to look at Dave. Okay, just a little…A bit more, and then again…

I don't manage to catch his eye, but the other employee at the counter notices me. She's probably wondering what I want. Oops. I dive back into my notes.

After ten minutes, I regret the whole thing. I bitterly regret coming here like this. For sending him a message that he hasn't even read yet and then showing up like this.

I decide to change tack. I throw all my things back in my bag. Except for one of them. I put my coat back on and head to the counter, bypassing the line. I reach my arm over the espresso machine and say loudly so he'll hear, "Here, I wanted you to be the first to have one."

Dave raises his head. Our eyes meet. That laughing-bewitching-irresistible look of his. He's glad I'm here, and I forget everything else. I am like a fish that's been thrown back into its pond.

He wipes his hands on a dish towel, grabs the book and, with a huge smile, says, "Oh, wow. Is this for me? *Radiant*. Very cool."

"Well, I know that self-care is a subject that really turns you on."

"Turns me on! In fact, I am very, very turned on by..."

"..."

"...self-care. It's good to see you."

We smile like two goofballs. Two goofballs alone in the world. I hold his gaze. It's sweet. The floor feels wobbly beneath my feet.

"And I thought you might be interested in my breakfast salad recipes."

I point to one of the images in the photo montage on the back of the book.

He looks at it more closely.

"Arugula before 9:00 a.m.? I don't think so, no... but I admit that I might be tempted by the secret to a 100 percent successful day of cocooning."

"Interesting."

"Mine are about 75 to 76 percent successful, which

is disappointing in the long run."

"Ooh, ouch. Yes. I can't even imagine!"

He puts my book on the counter. Quickly finishes making a giant latte which he hands to a customer before saying, "So what is the secret, then? Boosting your intestinal flora? Trusting in life?"

"Ah, I can't tell you. Otherwise it wouldn't be a secret."

He stares at me, amused. Grabs a portafilter, fills it with ground coffee and inserts it into the big espresso machine. He's very smooth. I'm proud to know him. He calmly presses a button and wipes his hands.

He points to my book.

"Are you going to sign it for me, I hope?"

I smile at him, show him all my teeth. Blush a little at the same time.

"If you want, except that means you'll be stuck with it…"

"Well, I hope so, Quinoa."

Okay, he's fucking irresistible.

I watch him finish serving customers. I can't believe we were totally naked together just a few days ago. That we made love. That we talked all night long. And that I'm standing here in front of him, my cheeks pink, not knowing how to behave. Feeling like a bit of a stranger, clumsy.

He motions for me to follow him to the back. We pass through a small kitchen and end up in a corner by the water heater in a room that vaguely looks like an office. He rummages around in an old tomato can filled with elastics, bread fasteners, screwdrivers and pointy things. Hands me a pen. Gives me a look that's a bit shy, impressed. Which just makes me want him even more.

I try to get hold of myself. I push aside the papers, sit on a corner of the table. I have to concentrate. I've never done this before, inscribed a book. If I ruin it I obviously can't just throw the book in the recycling.

I organize my face. I feel like laughing. I think that if Dave touched me right now, I'd pop like a champagne bottle.

I rest the book on my thighs.

"So. 'For Dave...'"

"Nah. I prefer 'For David Lanctôt.' Sounds more official. My mother will be proud."

"Well, okay, but you're not going to show this to your mother."

"I think we've known each long enough for me to introduce this to my mother. The book, I mean."

He smiles shyly. I blush some more. I try to act like I'm not finding this absolutely wonderful. As if I don't understand what it means for him to want to "introduce my book" to his mother. My heart is racing in all directions. I have to make a big effort to stay focused on the inscription. I won't get a second chance.

I write the first acceptable thing that comes into my head.

"Okay. 'For David Lanctôt, who is expressly forbidden from spilling orange macaroni and cheese with extra butter on this book. Happy reading!'"

Dave comes over. I feel his legs against my thighs. My belly feels warm.

"That's it? No little kisses?"

"Nope. Wouldn't dare in front of your mother."

"Aah. Okay. I understand. I guess I'll take them now, then."

He lifts the book out of my hands. I drop the pen when his fingers touch my neck and he gently holds my head. Turns it. Strokes my hair as he kisses me. On the mouth at first, and then on my neck. It feels good.

With a small smile, I unzip his jeans. He laughs, and so do I. He closes his office door with his foot. Takes my head in his hands to kiss me again, even better.

I wriggle out of my tights without breaking the moment. I'm pulling off the way-too-elasticy Lycra when it comes back to me.

Between kisses, I murmur, "Oh, um, I have to tell you something. I got engaged."

30,736 Likes

ellie_quinoa_forever The countdown has begun! My book *Radiant* is finally coming out on November 23. Find out all about it in my new YouTube video . . .! To mark the occasion, I'm launching the "15 days to become RADIANT" challenge. Every day I'll offer a new beauty & well-being tip to incorporate into your daily routine. See you tomorrow morning for the first challenge!

.

* CONTEST * I am giving away 10 VIP invitations to my launch. Every comment gives you a chance to win.

.

Link in bio to pre-order.

See all 3,764 comments

tania.soleil 15 DAYS ❤ I AM ABSOLUTELY PARTICIPATING!

mila.mongeau A princess!

roseamanda I really want to get a copy of your book please! I desperately need some motivation.

rebecka_cl Congratulations on the wedding OMG!

yasmena6899 Omg. You are too beautiful I fell in love with your YouTube channel. I could watch your videos at least a thousand times. Sam and you are the best.

cam_cam_cam @solange.veil Are you on board? A 15-day challenge, we're doing it! I want to be fit for Christmas!

alicemcmuffin Ellie, I'm going to buy your book! This is sick! Can't wait to try the recipes. You are so pretty.

étoilesdesmarais I love the dress so much! Where is it from???

maude_julie Wow wow and WOW! **#TeamEllie**

julia_aude Yas. I'm ordering right away. I've been waiting for this for a long time! ❤

labrie12 You're beautiful! You inspire me! Congratulations on your weight loss!

elainebilodeau You glow girl!

liam_HP Radiant, that describes you so well. What a beauty!

luanalu If this can make me look a little more like you, I will try it lol.

cynthiapelletier The cover is absolutely gorgeous. So inspiring Ellie.

françois lepage You are a sublime woman with an almost perfect body. Congratulations to you, DM me whenever you want.

juliette.romeo Hello Mrs. Samuel Vanasse ❤❤❤ **#Team Ellie&Sam**

chaton345 I like your vibe Ellie. Radiant and inspiring x 1000.

imjune I'm such a fan!!!!

books&cappuccinos Not really my style sadly.

felicite.proulx **@samantha.riri @marie-eve-pelletier**

marie-eve-pelletier Lol yuck! **@felicite.proulx**

Nat_from_the_block You look like you're 16! Too cute and adorable.

catherine.vd Impossibly beautiful!❤

10

Sitting at the kitchen island, I plan the posts for the "15 days to become RADIANT" challenge.

I'm trying hard, but...

I can retouch the photos in Light Studio, play around with my presets in PICTR, but even though Sam and I have already worked on them for hours, the pictures look like crap. I chew on my thumbnail while I scroll through them on my cell. I can't decide if the lighting is particularly bad or if I'm particularly ugly.

I sigh. My eyes pass from my book to my screen and from my screen to my book.

I don't look at all like the girl on the cover. My face is too round. My hair is too thin. My smile looks like it's pasted on. I look like a cheap imitation of myself...

Okay, don't panic. There's always a solution. I just have to find it.

In the meantime, I open my browser. Shop. It'll do me good to buy something. I type in the first thing that comes to mind. Glamora.com. Reading the product reviews relaxes me. I put anything that tempts me in my cart. A purifying cleanser that will "change your life." A "revolutionary" resurfacing serum. A radiance-boosting face mask that will "save the day." And, while I'm at it, "shine enhancing" lip gloss.

I click on my shopping cart. $232. Huh.

I take out the lip gloss. $218. Uh-huh. I try to remember the balance that I have to pay off on my credit card. Uh-huh. Yup. I think about the boxes of products that are piling up beside my desk. Okay. I close the tab. I can always come back to it later if I reconsider. (And I always reconsider.)

I make an effort to concentrate on my photos. Ughhhh. Focus, Ellie, focus.

I scroll through the images on my screen and I have a vision. The jar of peanut butter in the cupboard, second shelf on the left. Good grief, could I be hungry already?

Yes, I think so... Or not. It's not clear. Doesn't matter. Just a tiny spoonful.

I glance at the living room where Sam is composing. The coast is clear. I take the jar, a spoon and go back to my spot at the island.

Mistake. Big mistake. Three spoonfuls later, I'm regretting it, but I tell myself that at this point...

I get up, rummage around in my mason jars, find the mini chocolate chips well hidden behind the legumes. I sprinkle ten or so on top of my spoonful of peanut butter and swallow. It's a party in my mouth. I dig back in. Sprinkle. Five spoonfuls. Six. Seven.

No. I open the trash can and guiltily spit out the last one.

I need to love myself more than this. I can do it. I must be my own best friend. Why am I not capable of being my best friend? Spend less, eat less, meditate more.

I quickly rearrange the jars. Wash my spoon. Brush my teeth. Drink a big glass of water.

Then decide that I have no choice. I download Face Optimizer. I promised myself I would never do this, but it's temporary. Just this once. Just until I get fit again, get disciplined. Get back in the right state of mind that I was in six months ago.

I reach for my book. Put it in front of me to compare. I select one of the photos for the contest. The one I'll publish first. I zoom in. Start to edit. It's easy. I've already watched plenty of tutorials on YouTube. I reproduce the proportions to match my body on the cover. Accentuate my waist, just a little. A little more. And just a teensy bit more. I fine-tune my thighs to balance everything out. My arms. Hollow out my cheeks a bit because at this point…

You have to pay attention to the lines in the background because that's a dead giveaway — a distorted doorframe, a warp in the kitchen counter. The one thing that can't happen is…that I get caught.

But as long as we're here, I smooth out my skin, reduce my dark circles, brighten my eyes.

Ah. That's better. Much better.

Good. One down. Fourteen to go. I promise myself I will never do this again. Promise myself I'll lose the weight for real. That it's the end of the chocolate chips. My launch is in fifteen days. I have fifteen days.

Tomorrow I'll be back in the right mindset.

Tomorrow.

PAPA

It's July, and hot. I'm fifteen years old. The family is playing Scrabble. There's a bag of barbecue chips on the table. My mother has put out a small bowl for me. She's counted out ten chips. Ten chips, just for me. She makes a note in my food diary. Four points.

I'm on a diet. My mother and I are doing it together. I get twenty-eight points a day. Each thing that I eat has a certain number of points. Everything has to be counted, weighed, measured, controlled. My father and my sister are eating their chips straight from the bag. Unlimited chips for them but not for me. I'm the defective one. I have to count my chips.

While everyone is concentrating on the game, moving their letters around, I eat my ration. I've been waiting for this since noon. I've saved up all day. No butter on my toast, no dressing on my salad, no snack before dinner. I've promised myself that I would wait until the middle of the game before eating, but it's impossible to concentrate on anything else once the bowl is in front of me. I try to make them last. I break each one in half. I let each piece melt in my mouth.

E-A-T-I-N-G. I want to savor it, try to chew for as long as possible, but I swallow too fast. They disappear. All that's left behind is the orange dust on my fingertips. I lick them, suck them.

B-A-R-B-E-C-U-E. I look at the game board, but I'm thinking of something else.

C-H-I-P-S. Just one more, one last one.

C-R-U-N-C-H-Y. After that I'll stop. While my mother gets a double-word score and my sister adds up her points, I quietly stretch out my arm and take one chip from the bag.

My father sees me. His eyes are hard, but he doesn't say anything.

I eat it quickly and return to my letters.

M-O-R-E.

No.

No one's looking.

No.

Focus, Élisabeth, focus.

I sneak another. My father sees me, loses patience, gestures to me to pass him the bag. I obey. He puts it on his knees out of my reach. He is the self-proclaimed guardian of the chips.

"That's enough," he says.

My mother suggests that I eat cherry tomatoes instead, maybe some cucumber slices.

I am furious. Humiliated. I want to leave, but I have no place to go.

I get up, leave the game, climb the stairs, shut myself in the bathroom, kneel in front of the toilet, stare at the bottom of the bowl.

How do you do it, make yourself throw up? I want to be able to. Wish that it came naturally to me. I think it's high time. I read somewhere that girls do it with their toothbrush.

If I do it, my father will realize he went too far. If I do it, I'll get really thin for sure — so thin that he'll worry. I'll be skin and bones. He'll be sorry, but I'll be happy. Happy to be slim, of course. I'll no longer be invisible at school. In September, every-thing will start going my way, just like in the movies.

I take out my toothbrush, push it down my throat. Nothing. Just the minty taste in my nose, on my lips. I take it out, stick two fingers down instead. Stroke the strange little lumps at the base of my tongue.

My stomach heaves. My fingers in my mouth taste like salty burning. I want to throw up hard so that everyone hears. So they run upstairs and ask me to stop but it won't work because I won't stop.

I stick my fingers farther back, right to the back of my palate, and press down. I gag in small jerks. An earthquake on a human level. Nine point five on the Despair scale.

But nothing comes up. Nothing.

It takes a long time, it hurts, you have to hang on and fight for it. It's coming...you have to put up with the suffering just a bit longer, but...no.

I give up.

I can't follow a diet. Throwing up is too hard. If only I was stronger. If only I was at least able to vomit, to make myself sick, maybe my father would love me a bit more.

I stretch out between the toilet and the bathtub. I would give anything to be normal, to be able to eat chips from the bag.

I cry. For a long time. I hug the bath mat. Bury my face into it. It's pink and rough. I cry a bit harder so they'll hear me downstairs. So someone will come and save me, take me away from my sadness.

But no. I remain alone. The more I cry, the more I want to cry. I wait, I call myself names. I want them to know I don't like myself, either.

"I'm fat, ugly, disgusting, the worst person in the world. I hate myself. I'm going to kill myself."

I want them to understand, I want to tell them! *I hate myself, I hate myself so you don't have to, more than you can ever hate me, so you'll love me instead but no one does.*

I wait, clutching my fluffy life preserver, my terry cloth lifesaver.

But no one comes. Nobody. I am alone with my sadness, and it is swallowing me whole.

It swallows me up.

David Lanctôt has sent you a message

D: It's not yet clear to me. Are you going to invite me to the wedding?

E: HAHAHA. It depends, are you up for doing some dishes?

E: OK, this conversation is very wrong. But really, it was cool to see you! I like visiting your back office, if you know what I mean ;) Want to do it again?

E: Wow, I realize that my last message was 100% awkward . . . When I said back office, I didn't mean . . . Anyway, you know what I mean.

E: And don't say it!

E: Or not??? You're gone?

E: OK, bye then!

E: XX

E: Two X's or three? I don't know anymore! Anyway.

E: xxx

11

I woke up and there it was. There was nothing I could do about it.

Depression stomped on my heart like a baby bird hitting a too-clean window. A horrible feeling. Heavy.

I look at my cell on my way to the bathroom. Nothing from Dave. I go pee while I scroll. I take off my slippers. Stand on the scale.

I sigh. Put my slippers back on.

I drag myself to the kitchen. I can't find the energy to steam vegetables so I eat a crummy piece of toast with jam and go to crash in the living room. Disappointed.

I sit in my huge designer beanbag chair and stare at my green plants for five minutes. I think I'm over-watering my succulents. On the couch, Sam is playing the guitar in his underwear. I tell myself I have to post my photo for the contest. The challenge of the day: "Go out and get some air." I should do that, too, but I don't feel like it. I sink down into my chair a bit more.

Beside me, Sam plays the opening chords of the Rolling Stones' "Wild Horses." He stops to take a sip of coffee, then sings the opening lines without the guitar, just his voice: *"Childhood living / Is easy to do…"*

With a faint smile, he runs his hand through his hair. Keeps singing while looking me right in the eye to make me smile. To make me feel good.

"You know I can't let you / Slide through my hands." He looks away and plays a few chords.

I am captivated by Sam. I would like to look away, do something else, but it's impossible. I remain mashed into my chair, my eyes glued to him like a limpet. *"Wild horses couldn't drag me away."*

He sings the simple tune and it overwhelms me. The softness of his voice. His supple hands on the strings. I remember why I fell in love with him. I mean, how could you *not* fall in love with him. This gorgeous guy who plays the guitar. That almost arrogant look of a dude who doesn't really need you. Who doesn't need anything, in fact. Who's enough and completely whole all on his own.

I breathe in deeply, and an infinite heaviness fills my belly. I sink deeper into the pouf. I sink into the magma of polystyrene microbeads, incapable of resurfacing.

A tear emerges. It rolls down my cheek. I don't

know what it's doing there. It's lost on my face, while I sit there like a total asshole, watching Sam being the most beautiful, the most perfect thing in the world.

Wild horses couldn't drag me away.

He looks at me, lets the last note of the song fade away quietly, then puts down his instrument. Kneels in front of me and strokes my shoulder.

"Are you thinking about your father?" he asks softly.

I nod. It's so easy. Lying has become so easy.

His eyes are filled with sympathy.

"I'm sorry, Ellie. Such a shit time for you..."

He takes my head and places it against his chest. Holds me in his arms. It's been a long time since I've breathed in his scent, felt his skin on mine. I miss what it used to be like. It was so easy before.

The heaviness in my chest becomes almost unbearable. It grows, spreads, takes over.

"It's going to be okay, bunny," he whispers. "I'm here. I'm here."

My eyes close, my body slumps against his. I'm trembling. My jaw is clenched. I try to push down what is trying to come out.

But it doesn't work.

He rocks us both.

"Sam?" I say.

"Hmm."

"I think I'm in love with someone else."

12

I texted Alice to let her know I was coming. She didn't answer. Since it's not 10:00 a.m. yet, I guess she's still sleeping. Even so, I knock gently on the door three times.

Nothing.

I try a second time, tapping out a rhythm. I haven't decided whether it's more or less annoying to tap out a beat instead of your classic knock-knock.

Still nothing. Too bad.

I have no choice. I ring the bell. I wait. Ring again.

It's Opale who opens the door — a roommate not particularly gifted with human warmth. She's wearing a T-shirt from Maine that's just like my sister's. Her hair is all over the place. She does not look thrilled to see me.

Then again, she never looks thrilled to see me.

She sighs.

"Excuse me," I say. "I know the sun doesn't rise here before noon, but I've come to see Alice. It's important."

Opale stares at me without budging. Behind her I hear Alice come running.

"Ellie? What? What's happened, Jesus. Is Papa okay?"

My sister appears in the doorway. Completely naked. In her hand is a small piece of purple fabric.

She goes to pull it on and realizes it's a thong. I guess she was intending to wear more substantial underwear. She shrugs, snaps the elastic of her tiny undergarment against her thighs.

I look at her, practically naked. Too much information. She raises her eyes to the heavens, covers her breasts with her hands and motions for me to come inside.

"Yes. No, I…It's just…I've left Sam."

Whoa. Saying it out loud makes it way too official. My eyes fill with tears. Alice looks stunned.

"Oh, shit!"

"Yeah. I think I need a coffee. A strong one."

"No, bubbles. We need some bubbly!"

"Alice!"

"What?"

"Try not to be too sad."

I sit at the kitchen table, push around an old glued-together cup, little shooter glasses that stink of vodka and two or three plates full of croissant crumbs.

I lean my elbows on the table, my head in my hands.

I'm still stunned. I left Sam. I confessed everything, told him everything. It all seems unreal, impossible.

Alice fills the filter in the coffee machine from a family-sized tin of Queen Beans. She's pulled on a huge fleece. It would look great, if only it covered her bum.

Where is it written that I am obliged to be exposed to nude members of my family?

I'm starting to tell her that Sam was surprised, that he didn't cry, that he wasn't mad, that he just asked me to leave, when Opale walks behind her and gives her a little squeeze on her bottom.

Sweet Jesus. They sure are comfortable with each other for two roommates. Then Alice catches Opale by the waist, grabs her chin and kisses her on the mouth. It's noisy. I see the ends of their tongues. It lasts for an eternity. An eternity during which the light bulb finally goes on.

Opale isn't wearing a shirt like my sister's. She's wearing my sister's shirt. They were in the middle of having sex when I rang the bell. They're sleeping together.

I hear Opale whisper to Alice, "I'm going to have a shower. Do you want to come?"

Alice laughs, tilting her head in my direction. I smile to cover up my discomfort. To pretend like this situation isn't completely awkward.

I wait for Opale to close the bathroom door before I speak.

"You're sleeping with Opale!" I hiss.

"Yep."

"But weren't you on a sex sabbatical?!"

"This isn't sex."

"Oh, come ON, Alice! You're the worst quitter I've ever seen in my whole life."

"No, it's not about sex! We make love."

"LOL."

"Ellie, don't say LOL. It's not nice. Besides, it makes you sound like you're over thirty. I'm on strike for having sex with guys. That's what I meant when I said it last time. You misunderstood."

"Quitter."

The coffee machine makes a long gurgling sound.

"That means you have a girlfriend!"

"No, actually, she's not my girlfriend. We're not a couple."

"But you 'make love.'"

"We love each other. We just don't need a label."

"And Opale's okay with that?"

"I think so, we haven't officially talked about it yet but it seems pretty obvious I still don't want to get involved with someone."

I should have known that with Alice it's never simple. I must look a bit confused, because she says, "It's okay, just say it, that you think it's a 'phase.'"

"No, I don't think that."

"That you think I'm with a girl just to provoke Maman."

What? Where did that come from?

"Not that, either!" I shrug.

"If you think about it for two seconds, it's so constraining, the idea of sexual orientation. Why can't you just fall in love with another person? Regardless of gender or sex? A person, get it?"

"Yes, of course, obviously. I agree."

"Okay, well, if you obviously agree, then show it. Because I feel like you're judging me."

"Well, no, absolutely not. It's just that I don't understand why, given all the 'persons' in the world, you've chosen Opale...Admit it — she's...a little unpleasant. She couldn't smile even if her life depended on it."

She puts a mug in front of me and pours hot coffee.

"On the contrary, Opale is cool, I swear! It's just that with you...I don't know...milk?"

"No, thanks."

"Sugar?"

"No. With me what?"

"Cognac?"

"No! With me what?"

"Well...she just doesn't...get you."

"Ah. Swell."

"She has this grudge against influencers, and it's stronger than she is...You know."

"I don't know, actually."

"Anyway, tell me! You broke up with Sam, geez, I want to hear everything!"

David Lanctôt has sent you a message

D: OK, we need to talk. This has gone on long enough.

E: What???

D: I leafed through your book. You put chickpea flour in your chocolate chip cookies. Quinoa, some things are sacred, OK?

E: Hey! That's my signature recipe! You should try it, it's really really good. I'm not kidding.

D: Impossible. No way. Impossible.

E: You're defying me, David Lanctôt?

D: Cute. You really believe it.

E: You dare to challenge the god of chickpeas? Watch your ass or its evil winds will knock you out!

D: Did you seriously just make a fart joke?

E: Yup.

D: Adorable.

Samuel Vanasse has sent you a message

S: Meeting Monday 1 p.m. with Malik to plan what happens now.

E: Are you sure that's a good idea? There's no rush.

S: Yes. We are professionals, we'll act like it.

E: OK. I was saying that for you . . . Whatever you want.

S: Thank you.

13

Third night of sleeping on my sister's old speckled two-seater pastel couch. Third night of being woken up in the wee hours by her and Opale coming home from a party. Third night of listening to them "making love," laughing, eating cereal and "making love" again.

It's not an appropriate breakup soundtrack.

I'm depressed. Sam's right. There's no time to waste. I'm afraid of the consequences, but this is the twenty-first century, people, and I will prove I don't need to be in a relationship to succeed. Anyway, I can't do exactly what I blame Sam for doing, staying together just for show.

We're going to come up with a game plan. Announce our separation. We're going to have to put up with messages from grieving fans, articles in *Celebrity World*, the stupid comments, and after that I'll be able to move on to something else. Soothe my little heart. Work to reinvent myself.

Reinvent myself, buy some wine, and invite Dave for dinner.

Dave . . . I think about him all the time. It makes me dizzy but I think the important thing is to listen to your heart. The first step is trusting yourself...

That's beautiful. It makes me feel good. I should post that.

I search through my cell to find visuals that will fit. A matcha latte? No. Maybe the beach in Cahuita...

Oh! I made a time-lapse meditation video a few weeks ago. That would be perfect.

I'm in the middle of posting when Alice breezes into the living room.

"Hey," I say without looking up from my phone. "I forgot to tell you that Maman has gone backpacking in Mexico with Nico!"

"Yeah, already heard about it on Facebook, thanks."

"Sorry. A backpacking trip...next thing you know they'll be getting matching tattoos. No, even better, he'll introduce her to his parents! Can you imagine his mother's face? Yikes!"

I burst out laughing, but there's just dead silence from Alice. It's not like her. Usually she wastes no time making fun of Estelle.

I look up at her. She's eating a granola bar, completely dressed, her hair tied back, looking serious. It's weird.

"I'm going to pack boxes at Papa's. You should come."

"Boxes?"

"He's moving into the cottage. That's where he wants to…be at the end. There's also his office at the university to clear out if…"

"Oh…yes, I'd like to…but…I…I can't."

Alice crosses her arms, frowns, looks at me as if she's my babysitter and I've refused to eat my brussels sprouts. It's annoying.

"I have a meeting," I say, tapping on my phone. "But…"

"Don't mess around, Ellie. I know things aren't easy between you and Papa, but you won't have the rest of your life to sort it out."

"I know."

"Doesn't seem like it."

"I know…but I'm in the middle of a breakup here!"

"Sure."

"Besides, why is it up to me to 'sort it out'? That's not how it works."

"Oh, really? How does it work, then?"

"I don't know. I…don't know! Stop judging me!"

She puts a finger in front of her mouth. Inhales and then exhales calmly. She's being the mature one right now, and it sucks. I lie back on the couch with my back to her. Pull the blanket up to my chin and sulk as I examine the patterns on my speckled pastel fortress.

"Okay," she says behind me. "By the way, the girls are organizing a party. Maya's just paid off her credit card, and they want to celebrate. It doesn't bother me if you want to sleep here, but chances are they'll be getting out the karaoke machine..."

"Ouch. No thanks. I'll figure something out."

"Whatever you want."

Just what I need. To be homeless. Oh, joy.

"Alice, wait a minute!"

"Yeah?"

"Will Dave be there?"

14

"We broke up."

"Ellie broke up with me."

"I broke up with him."

"She also cheated on me."

Malik swallows his short espresso in a single gulp. Looks at me, looks at Sam, looks at the two of us again in disbelief.

"Yeah," I say, lowering my head. "I did...yeah."

I feel super guilty. Sam rubs his face with his hand, exhales loudly.

Malik taps his pen nervously, puts it down, then leans back in his chair.

The silence is deafening.

"But," I add, "it's not as if...You can't tell me, Sam, that you've never...cheated on me while you were on tour. You know, I'm not a fool, either, but now it doesn't matter anymore anyway..."

"Never," Sam says, stung. "I have not once slept with someone else since we've been together."

"Okay."

"..."

"But ... making out?"

"No!"

That surprises me. I mean, I still find it hard to believe, but Sam looks very serious. Almost insulted that I would even think it.

"Okay, well, groped, whatever ..."

"No! I would never do that, Ellie. Never."

"Okay, okay. Sorry."

I settle back in my seat, a little annoyed that I'm being made out to be the villain here. Our relationship is so much more complicated than that, it seems to me ...

I lower my head and mumble, "It's true that ... I mean, what would that have looked like ..."

"Pardon?"

"I'm just saying that you would never have compromised our perfect image as a perfect couple."

"Are you serious?"

"I don't know ... Maybe what really turns you on is our image."

"That's so unfair."

"And asking me to marry you live on YouTube is fair?"

Malik tries to say something, but Sam cuts him off.

"What are you talking about?"

"Well, let's see, in what kind of world do you think it's a good idea to ask your girlfriend to marry you in front of ten thousand people?"

"I don't know, but I...why did you say yes in the first place?"

"That's exactly the problem! Do you think I had any choice?"

Sam looks stricken. I've hurt him. I don't know what else to say. I'm starting to think it was a bad idea to come here so soon.

I take a deep breath.

"I'm sorry."

"..."

"You don't deserve this. I'm so sorry."

Sam nods slowly. After a long silence, he says, "You have no idea how much I love you, Ellie. No idea." His voice breaks. He looks right at me. His eyes are begging me to tell him that I love him, too. To give us a chance. But I can't do it.

He starts to blink. He frowns, sniffles. Quickly wipes away a tear — two — with the tips of his fingers. I would like to be able to leave him without leaving, without taking anything from him. I would leave him the old me. I would go and live with Dave in a parallel universe.

Malik steps in.

"My sweeties…existential crises are all fine and good, but we have to examine our timing here. Ellie, your book is coming out in two weeks. And then, your Christmas dinner will be on the front page of the next issue of *Femme*. By the way, the photos are magnificent, absolutely magnificent. That comes out at the end of the month…"

I don't hesitate for a second.

"Malik, I know it isn't ideal, and a lot of people are going to be turned off, and it might cost me a partnership or two, but…"

He makes a time-out sign with his hands, which annoys me.

"Separating isn't the kind of decision that you make on a whim. It would be a shame to spoil everything by acting too hastily. Who knows how the two of you might feel in a few days?"

"But you always say that I'm not relatable enough. Surely a breakup is relatable. Anyone can identify with that."

"Yes, except we need to face reality, Ellie. No one wants to hear about breaking up just before the holidays. No one."

"But…"

"Timing is everything."

"I've made my decision. I want to listen to my heart, do you understand?"

"Okay, fine. Perfect. Very good. Listen to your heart, my sweet. That's wonderful. Very beautiful."

He grabs a pile of papers on his desk, flips through them, puts them in order and slides them into a folder.

"Do you have an emergency fund?"

"A what?"

"A little cushion. Money to tide you over in the absence of contracts over the coming months. Sam has his music, but what about you?"

"N-no…"

"So I imagine that you're prepared to go back to basic partnerships? Ready-to-cook meals, party poppers, meal delivery apps, that kind of thing…"

"But that's hardly in the spirit of Quinoa Forever. Are you serious?"

"Very serious."

"I thought… I mean, I'm not giving up anything!

I'm going to work twice as hard. I think that I can still aim high, get great contracts, achieve my goals! I have lots of great content to offer!"

"Friendly advice, Ellie. Forget about making the top three this year. You are going to fall flat on your ass."

"No way!"

"Listen, it's your decision. But I warn you. This is not a good time."

He slips the file with the papers into his desk. Plants his elbows on the table and looks at us like he's wondering why we're still sitting in front of him. Clearly he is exasperated.

Clearly I am, too.

"I understand! But it's not enough to stay together just for the contracts!"

"No, of course not. But you can give yourself a bit of time. Consider carefully."

"Time?"

"Yes. Let's talk about it after Christmas. If you are still happy with your decision, we'll wait and announce after Valentine's Day."

"Valentine's Day?"

Malik pulls out the folder that he has just shoved in the drawer, opens it and starts to line up the papers in front of us. I go through them and nervously start chewing on my thumbnail.

"February is a big month," he says enthusiastically. "Offers are on the table and they're juicy ones! Five, ten, twenty thousand dollars. It's up to you to decide, but there's enough here to see you through the coming months."

"Or…"

"If Quinoa Forever is truly important to you, Ellie, you need to protect your brand. Make some calculated decisions."

On the desk there are proposals for romantic getaways, flowers, jewelry, lubricants, chocolate…I am overwhelmed.

I take a deep breath and turn to Sam.

"What do you think?" I ask.

His eyes are empty, his head down.

"I'll do what you want."

He's soft, expressionless. I've never seen him like this. It throws me.

"But if it were up to you, what would you do?" I say softly.

"If it were up to me, we would stay together."

It's my turn to lower my head guiltily. I look at my

hands. I've chewed on the skin around my thumb so deeply that it's bleeding.

"I think Malik is right," Sam says. "It would be better to wait."

I turn to Malik. "How will we keep it quiet?"

"Do exactly as before. Exactly. And then, at the beginning of March, *at the latest*, we break your news. Your paths are diverging, you are more friends than lovers, you remain on good terms, you will continue to collaborate in the future...you know the drill."

"Mmmm-hmmm."

"And until then, you continue to post. Sunday brunch, small moments from your everyday life and all the usual things."

I look at Sam. He gives me a sad little smile, nods his head a bit.

"Okay," I say. "But the end of February. At the latest."

Malik throws me a satisfied look. I don't know what to think. I tell myself that we are just acting like professionals. This is the thing to do, isn't it?

"Okay, off you go," he says. "Make us dream a little more. One last lap around the track, my little tigers!"

LIVE AUTHENTIC

For a long time I've thought that authenticity is the part of you that endures above everything else. The thing that remains once you take away the desire to be loved, to make money, to please others, or just the desire to shine in general. The part of you that is untouchable and absolute.

This may be true on paper, but practically speaking, I wonder what makes my actions, my gestures authentic? The fact that they're spontaneous? Thoughtful? Shared? Unique? Their strength or their pliability? Is it authenticity that interests me, or what I get out of it?

Because if authenticity exists, the opposite also exists. So what does it mean to be inauthentic? I mean, if my desires, my fears, my needs, my relationships, my experiences — if all those things influence me and change me, what is real and what is false? What does it mean to be yourself?

I read #liveauthentic, #beauthentic, #seekauthenticity and I wonder what that means. Does it mean always listening to your heart, to your feelings? I try, but what I want is often contradictory. I may believe in the importance of honesty, and still be afraid of the consequences if I tell the truth. I may want to collaborate with other YouTubers, but also feel like I'm in competition with them. Want something and the exact opposite, be one thing and the opposite.

When you think about it, just the idea of trying to be more authentic feels like something that actually springs from a fundamental lack of authenticity. Maybe authenticity is a fiction. A marketing fiction. The promise of a better life stripped of all complexity, filled with pure emotions and true feelings. A part of yourself that evolves on the margins of the world, untouchable, unchangeable.

We're offended by influencers' lack of authenticity, by their alleged hypocrisy. We call them out, ridicule them. For instance, I'm thinking about someone who would say they're worried about the environment on the one hand and then promote an oil company on the other, or who wants to be everyone's best friend on YouTube but who yells at a taxi driver on Instagram. People take real pleasure in exposing "inauthenticity" and denouncing it. We want to believe that there is such a thing as the disinterested and magnanimous influencer — influencers who are truly "authentic." When in fact, the image that I project of myself is very calculated, has been infinitely honed. I put myself on display, on stage. It's a publicity show above anything else. Even when it looks spontaneous, even when I appear to be vulnerable, I am always two people, contradictory. True and false at the same time. I am both the story and the author of the story.

The truth is complicated.

15

I came back to the apartment with Sam. He didn't say a word during the entire ride home.

When I get there, I see the little welcome mat that says Home Sweet Home. It's crooked, dirty. I realize that there is not a place on earth that I would find more depressing than right here.

Sam shuts himself up in the living room. I decide to go into the bedroom. My heart sinks when I walk in. It's like a small museum of our failed relationship. The unmade bed, the smell of shampoo and dampness. Our clothes lying around in small messy piles. Our things. Like witnesses to a time when what was mine was his and what was his was mine. The stolen T-shirt that I wore as a nightie, the love notes on Post-its covered in dust. The tacky mug received as a gift, the travel photos, the lip balm we shared.

I need to do some housekeeping. Hide our things in a grocery bag. Throw them into the back of the closet where they won't mean anything anymore.

Once I've tidied up, I join Sam in the living room with my calendar app open. I have the firm intention of organizing our "new life." I want to plan the coming weeks. It will be good to plan.

Hugging his guitar, he's consoling himself by playing songs pulled from the repertoire of his band, Monday — "Somebody to Love," "Unbroken."

I politely let him finish. Listen as I look up at the cracks in the ceiling.

"Don't you know I was made for lovin' you, hon. I've never learned to lose you. Should have known better."

He really knows how to tear at your heartstrings. Okay, so I feel bad, but at the same time, let's not pretend. I know he wrote these songs for his ex. A girl in Vancouver he dated for three months, two years ago.

I think about Dave. His smile, his soft eyes. I daydream. At least, I'd like to, but Sam's trembling voice in the background is unnerving.

"I can lie and say I'm all right. I can lie and say I'm unbroken. But I ain't, babe, I ain't."

I decide to interrupt his flight of lyricism.

"So, you want to take the living room and I'll take the bedroom? Switch? How do you want to…how?"

"When did you stop loving me, Ellie?"

"I…I don't know, I…"

"That guy, the coffee man. Are you really in love

with him? As fast as that? How do you know for sure?"

"Sam, we're not going to talk about that…"

"So what is it? He does things that I don't?"

Sam stares at me, serious. It is super uncomfortable to see him in this sad, pathetic state.

"No, really, explain it to me!" he adds. "What does he do that I don't? Because I don't get it."

He's waiting for an answer. But I am vibrating. For real. My phone is buzzing in my hand. It's Mila. I refuse to answer. Turn off the ringer and throw my phone on the footstool.

As gently as possible, I say, "Sorry, what were we talking about? Yeah, so how do you want to do this? It's no problem for me to take the sofa."

"Okay, and what about if I have a date?"

His question takes me by surprise. I haven't thought about it. Does it bother me that he's already thinking about that? The same person who seemed so devastated fifteen seconds ago? Okay, I get it, who am I to begrudge him right now?

"I can go to Alice's," I say. "Just…let me know a little ahead of time."

"Perfect." He's getting ready to start singing again.

"It's not that it bothers me," I say. "But our breakup has to be kept a secret for a while yet, so I guess we can't date, can we?"

"But what about you? Are you going to keep seeing Mr. Single Espresso?"

Sam's acting like a six-year-old who's just lost a dodgeball game. I hear my phone buzzing on the footstool.

"No! Well...I don't know. Maybe."

"So how are you going to do that?"

"I'll be discreet."

"And so will I. I'll be discreet, too."

I want to say that it's more risky for him than for me, but my cell is vibrating again.

I take a look. Another call from Mila Mongeau, which is weird. We've never done that, talked on the phone. The telephone — it's so...intrusive.

"Do you want to take the couch from Thursday to Sunday and every other Wednesday?" Sam asks.

More ringing. Three calls in five minutes. Two text messages that tell me to call her, so it must be important. Maybe I'm still in trouble or whatever.

I signal to Sam that I'm sorry, but I have to answer.

"Hello? What's happening?"

"Hey-hey, Ellie, it's Mila. I have this *amazing* project to propose to you. I'm over the moon. And when I tell you I have your back, you'd better believe me. Are you ready? You're ready! Three words: New Year's Festival."

"…"

"We're going to New Year's Festival!!!"

"Mila," I say impatiently. "That's in Australia, I —"

"New Zealand."

"Sorry, but I really don't have the money right now to go to New —"

"You don't get it! Banana Apparel is sending me to the festival with a friend of my choice. We're going to produce content for their spring-summer collection. Can you believe it!"

Red alert. Any plan of Mila's is suspicious. If it seems too good to be true, it is too good to be true. At the same time, going to New Zealand right now would be unbelievable. No one would ask me if I want to sleep on the couch in New Zealand.

I look over at Sam. I signal to him that I won't be much longer. I try to think quickly.

At the other end of the line, Mila's getting impatient.

"I can always ask Jordanne if you want."

"No! No, it's tempting, for sure. I just need to . . .
check on . . . one little thing with Malik first."

Check one little thing or do a thorough investiga-
tion, depending.

"Yay!" she says, super cheerful. "I've got an invitation for the opening of a new eyebrow bar in Mile
Ex tomorrow aft. Come with me and I can tell you
all about the gig in more detail."

"Uh . . . okay, let's do that."

"Perfect. I'll send you the deets. Bye, girl!"

I hang up and it hits me. Did she just say eyebrow
bar? A bar for eyebrows? What?

At this exact moment, lying on the couch, his eyes
full of tears, Sam says it again.

"When did you stop loving me?"

Text messages between Ellie and Alice

E: So, Dave???

A: He said he would drop by.

E: NICE.

E: OK, but you didn't say I was going to be there, did you?

A: No. I did what you said.

E: You are the best.

Text messages between Mila and Ellie

M: Tomorrow 2 p.m. at Browz. Beaubien and Park. Give them my name when you get there.

E: Got it. See you tomorrow. Xx

16

I pack my bag for the night, all set to face an evening of karaoke at Alice's. Underwear, toothbrush, makeup, deodorant, dry shampoo, healthy snacks, change of clothes, pj's, warm socks. The basics.

It weighs a ton. My heart is pounding when I walk through the door of my sister's apartment around 10:30. I drop my things under the coatrack in the hall. The mythical coatrack. I think about the night I saw Dave for the first time. Our debate about the word "pretzel." The cushion jokes.

What were the odds, I ask myself. What were the odds that we would meet by the coatrack? I could have left five minutes earlier. He could have come wearing a hoodie. Three degrees warmer out and he wouldn't have needed a coat. There was a high probability that we would each live out our lives without ever seeing or talking to each other. He would have come to Alice's that night. Would have walked past the coatrack without stopping. I would have already left. End of story.

How many life-changing human beings do we walk by every day? A lot. So for Dave and me, it could have been something like fate. I mean, if it's not fate, if it's just chance, then the fleeting randomness of those moments is unbearable. Unbearable. (Note to self: These phrases would make great captions for a post.)

I try to contain my excitement as I make my way through the dense crowd piled into Alice's living room. Standing on top of a coffee table made from recycled wooden pallets, Maya and Opale are performing "Dancing Queen" with a great deal of enthusiasm. Feather boas around their necks, their eyes like disco balls.

When she sees me, Alice bounces over. Spills a bit of her rum and Coke on my sweater.

"Ellie, this is a big night!" she cries, hanging on my neck.

"Oh, my God, no! Shush!"

I try to get her to lower her voice, throw a few worried looks around us. She takes a step back, raises her arms in the air and starts to dance like a bird about to take off.

"There's looooove in the air!" she shouts, laughing.

"Shut up, Alice!"

"Relax. Your lover boy isn't even here yet."

I grab her gently by the shoulders.

"I'm not here for him! I just didn't want to stay home. It's too depressing."

Okay, I admit — that's all baloney, half truths, fake news. Seriously, though, the last thing I want is for Dave to think I'm chasing him. I don't want to rush anything. I want him to think I'm here by accident. That it was just made to be, the two of us.

Alice grabs me by the chin.

"You're so uptight, Ellie. You know what you need?"

She squeezes my cheeks with her big soft hand. Her pupils are dilated like beach balls.

Ah, I get it. She's on something, taken a pill. It's just like the night I met Dave. The karaoke, the crowd, the drugs. It's all exactly the same — except this time I'm free.

I start to smile uncontrollably.

"Alice, you are completely stoned!"

"No, listen to me. This is serious. Listen, listen to real advice. You know what would do you good?"

"What?"

"To sing!"

"I don't think so."

"I've never heard you sing! Sing!"

"No."

"Siiiinng! Who cares, siiiinng! Be free, you are free, Ellie! Sing!"

"NO."

"Have a drink, then."

She hands me her huge cocktail in a vintage plastic glass and, not giving me any choice, butts it up against my lips and pours it into my mouth too fast. It runs down my chin while I try to contain the overflow by taking big gulps.

The glass is empty. My sweater is damp. Rum and Coke runs down between my breasts.

The music stops. Everyone in the room hears Alice say, "Ellie, let loose!"

I see Opale and Maya stumble down off the stage. Alice drops her glass and grabs my arms. Leads me toward the karaoke machine, shoves a gold mic in my hands and forces me up onto the table by pushing on my bum.

I resist weakly. Everyone is looking at us.

The screen in front of us displays "Quand on est en amour" by Patrick Norman.

"El-lie! El-lie! El-lie!" Alice cries, clapping her hands.

I signal for them to stop the machine. That I'm not going to do it. This isn't my song. But every eye in the room is on me. I beg her to put on my song. I have a karaoke song that I practice from time to time.

In front of me the progress bar for the new song loads with astonishing speed — 20%, 30%, 40%.

"Alice, it's not in the right key. I can't just sing in any key!"

She's not listening. Just waves her arms in the air as if to say, "Fly, fly, use your wings, my child."

The progress bar is at 60%. I meet Opale's sarcastic glance at the other end of the room. She's leaning against the doorframe, and I'm guessing she loves the idea of me crapping out because I'm too scared. I imagine she can't wait to tell her friends about it in some ironic discussion group on Messenger.

That gets me fired up. I'll show her. The progress bar is at 80%. I'll show her that not only am I capable of singing, but I can also be quite talented when I put my mind to it.

I run my hand through my too-thin hair, toss it back in what I hope is a feisty gesture.

Progress bar at 100%.

Dave is here.

I hear three little bells.

I'm on.

"*Si tu crois*..."

Shit. Dave is here! I miss the beginning of the song, the words turn from turquoise to mauve. I quickly catch up with the lyrics, but I'm singing too low. I try to sing a bit higher. Too high.

I'm singing about how love has let me down!

I can't find the key. My voice is thin and strained. My eyes lift from the screen to Dave, from Dave to the screen. I see that he sees me. That he realizes that the pathetic singer with the quavery voice is me.

I stumble over the line about how the sun is going to come out again and realize that Dave is here with a girl. Dave has come with a date. I've seen her somewhere, a tall brunette. I've seen her before. He's resting his hand on her back. Talking to her, all relaxed and easy.

The more I sing, the more I slip away from the song. Away from the notes to somewhere else. To another song. Which one, I don't know.

Laurence, Florence...

Florence Marquis!

How the fuck do I know her name? She likes toast. Traditional film photography. She wears big hats. Her dog's name is Fabrice.

I've already stalked this person. Who is she?

I hear the three little beats before the chorus.

"Ne laisse pas passer
La chance d'être aimé..."

The backup vocals fly to my rescue for the chorus. But it's too late, girls. Where were you a minute ago?

From the other end of the room, Dave sneaks a peek at me and then returns to his conversation. I see Florence run her hand through his hair. She kisses him on the neck, then on the mouth.

He laughs happily. And I'm singing about how your heart becomes less heavy when you're in love.

Less heavy, my ass. I know who she is, this Florence. He went to Thailand with her. They went camping in Bic. Ate lobster rolls on Thanksgiving.

Florence is his ex.

No more sounds come from my mouth. I stand there like a statue. My broken little karaoke queen heart has just left the building.

I get down from the table, hand my mic to some guy, leave to find a quiet corner. Walk through the kitchen, rush to the bathroom, turn off the light and close the door. I try to calm myself down and curl up in a little ball on the damp bath mat. I bury my face in the deep, fluffy warm pile. Gravity overwhelms me. Alone on my polyester island, I weep stupid tears.

Dave is not in love with me.

17

9:12 a.m. The sun is up, I'm chilling with my only friend — the speckled pastel two-seater sofa. A ray of sunlight breaks through the crack between the curtains, hits my cheek and tickles my eyelids.

I open my eyes.

No. Memories of yesterday come flooding back.

No. One at a time. Gouging out each one of my synapses.

No.

I flash back to the disaster. First, I lock myself in the bathroom. Someone knocks on the door, calling my name. I open it and come face-to-face with Opale. She says she saw everything, that she understands. That Alice is too stoned to come and help me. She leads me to her room beside the kitchen. Asks me if I'm okay. Says that I can stay there and wait. That I can always sleep on the couch.

This is the first time, I think — the first time that she has ever been nice to me.

I wait. Fifteen, twenty, thirty minutes, I don't know. I stink of rum. I hear the noises of the party, the laughing, the music. I feel ridiculous hiding away in a little ball on Opale's bed. It smells like stale cigarettes.

But to go out, chat — that would take more strength than I can muster.

The door opens three times. Each time I think it's going to be Dave. That he's come looking for me.

But no. Each time, someone sees me, gives me an apologetic look and then leaves.

At one point I hear his voice near the door. He laughs, talks about two grilled hot dogs. I imagine him finding me here, seeing me like this.

I can't stay here. This whole business is pathetic. I need to leave, find my bag, go back home.

I visualize my way out. I can do it. I'm going to do it.

I wait until things are quiet in the kitchen. I smile at myself in the mirror to see whether it looks convincing.

Never mind. I go through the drafty kitchen, step around the sweaty bodies in the living room, make my way through the clusters of people in the hall...

And run smack into Dave at the door.

Shit. He's completely alone, wearing his coat.

"Hey, Quinoa."

I freeze. He's watching me. Trying to read me.

I hesitate slightly.

"Hi, how are you?"

I give him the same hi-how-are-you that I'd give to a delivery person or the spin instructor at the gym. A hi-how-are-you that says I am a nice friendly girl but that's the extent of it because we don't know each other well and will never play a big role in each other's lives.

"Everything okay?"

"Yup! Goodnight."

I motion for him to step aside to let me pass. Pick up my bag under the coatrack. The bag carrying my pajamas that I was going to wear when I went to sleep at his place. Taking pajamas, who does that? I am so clueless.

I look for my coat.

"Ellie, what's going on?"

I turn around. And realize that he has no fucking clue.

I want to leave.

"Are you kidding me?" I ask.

He grabs my forearms, surprised. His hands are warm, his look tender.

"Talk to me," he says.

I melt. I give in. I want to bury my arms in his coat and press myself against him. I would be tiny next to his hugeness.

"Is it because of Florence?" he asks.

He's kind of talking to me like I'm a child. It seems like he finds this cute. That it's cute that I'm mad.

On the inside, I'm folding like a soft crêpe. Only my shell, my pride, is left standing in front of Dave.

"Well. It's just that... I wonder why you came with her. It's totally fine that you see other girls or whatever, it's your life. But like, I don't understand why you invited her to my sister's. In my face. That's all."

He's pressing his lips together, thinking about what to say. I'm afraid, so I keep talking.

"Like," I say too fast, "the other day, we made love in your office and now you're here with another girl, and it's weird. But I don't want you to feel bad, I just..."

"Made love."

He says it smiling, like he's flattered and surprised at the same time. He obviously didn't think of it the same way. Ouch, agh, no. Quick. Back up. Regroup.

"I meant we fucked. I just don't find that a super nice word, myself, but…it's just that I meant at least warn me ahead of time and I won't come. Do whatever you want, that's great, but I don't want to know. I don't want to be there, you know?"

I'm talking without looking at him. Without pausing for a breath. Without listening to myself. Too busy trying to spare us both this awkward moment. To cover up the fact that I've been reading our situation wrong. All wrong.

"Ellie," he says, "I apologize. I wasn't thinking… I'm so sorry."

I can't believe he thinks saying that is going to make me feel better. That he wasn't thinking. That I'm not even part of the equation. Not for one second.

I hear Florence's voice behind me. It's not the voice I imagined. More nasal. More piercing, too. She says she's ready to leave.

I smile, turn around, wish them a good evening, pretend to be making my way to Alice's room. I walk trying to fix my gaze on something — the ceiling, the baseboards — anything to help me stay upright.

He's ruined it all — the coatrack, the cushions.

131

He's ruined destiny. Everything is ugly now. Everything is ugly, random, unbearable.

End of story.

9:16 a.m. Back in the nightmare of speckled pastel, I see the credits rolling on the flashback that's been running on a loop since last night. Camera work by me. Sound recording by me. Script really not by me.

Lying alone on the couch, I contemplate the emptiness, the hole that has opened up in the middle of my chest. That's growing.

I thought he was into me. That he saw me. Me, only me. I promise myself that I will win him. I haven't been at my best, but I will do better. Make him see me fresh, as someone who's shiny and irresistible. So he falls head over heels in love. So he'll regret having been so slow to understand that I'm the one he needs. The only one he needs.

9:24 a.m. The apartment is completely silent. Just the low hum of life carrying on. I wrap myself up in my cold comforter and replay the sad bits from yesterday evening. Play them back to myself while I cry, trying not to make too much noise. Bawl my eyes out until I lose touch with reality.

Until I hear murmurs coming from Opale's room.

Whispers that become moans. Moans that turn into cries of passion. Alice makes funny noises.

I bury my head in my cushion. Sleep. Disappear.

@laflorencemarquis

– A photo of her unmade bed.
– Road trip. The car window half open, her face in the rearview mirror.
– A dog named Fabrice.
– Crouched in bike shorts in front of a round mirror resting on the ground, a photo of her moving day.
– A beige mushroom.
– Patio chairs.
– A black-and-white self-portrait. Blurry.
– Wash drying on a clothesline.
– Smoked salmon and radishes on a slice of rye bread.
– Her knees. Torn jeans, leather boots.
– A novel by Virginia Woolf. A cup of coffee.
– Stretched out on the kitchen table, she's wearing a long dress and eating a cheeseburger.
– Her eye.
– Her bare arms. Her face covered by a hat.
– Shadows on a concrete wall.
– Video of the wind in her hair. Her face barely visible. Her full lips.
– A seat belt across her hips, across her breasts.

– Her foot in a dad shoe. An orange sock. An ankle bracelet.

– Behind the scenes at a photo shoot. She's the photographer.

– Polaroids of her bare legs.

– A bowl of spaghetti with tomato sauce. A bottle of red.

– Raindrops on a window.

– Close-up of her navel above her jeans.

– A motel.

– Grainy image. White bathing suit. Nipples.

– Takeout.

– Footprints in the mud.

– Prosciutto, figs and ricotta on multigrain.

– A magazine open to a collage in beige and white.

– Dave from the back, making coffee.

– A rumpled sleeping bag.

– Two cups of coffee in a car cupholder.

– Her stomach peeking through an unbuttoned white shirt, green panties.

– In sandals with baggy pants, her arms crossed over her breasts.

– Dave. A lobster roll. The ocean.

18

11:36 a.m. My speckled pastel hideaway. I've checked
my accounts. Answered my messages. Posted my challenge for the day: "Reinvent your morning routine."
I won't comment on that because it's ridiculous.
I am ridiculous. I scrolled, glued to my phone like a
leech, hoping for a little consolation. Found none,
but I bought one hundred and fifty dollars' worth
of supplements. Vitamins, marine collagen, adapt-
ogens, the whole nine yards. I am exhausted. I get
up, move my feet as far as the kitchen where Opale
and Maya are making French toast and listening to
the radio. Talk radio, which gives me a headache.
I sit down and lean my head on my folded arms. My
chest still smells of rum.

Shower. I need to shower.

"Can I get you something?" I hear Opale ask,
her voice dripping with sarcasm. "A turmeric latte?
Green smoothie? Glass of rosé?"

Maya stands in front of the stove and snorts with
laughter. I lift my head, rub my eyes.

"I'll have coffee if there is any. Please."

I watch her pour me a coffee with one hand and

ruffle her curls with the other.

I remember Alice's words. *She doesn't get you.*

I try to make myself very small. I wish my sister would hurry and get up. Sitting here all alone without her, I feel like a stranger, out of place. Like a pair of white sneakers that are still too white.

Maya flips the French toast and sings something from *Mamma Mia*. Shades of yesterday evening. Opale sings along with a wooden spatula in her hand. They do this thing with their voices — sing in harmony. It's sweet. Maya dances with her arms in the air. They know all the words by heart. It's impressive, the way they bond with each other. I've never had that with anyone. I think it would be nice.

I quietly applaud. They turn around looking a little embarrassed, but don't say anything. They just continue making breakfast in silence.

I notice Opale's sweater, a cotton hoodie with KALE on the front in big green letters.

I smile. It's just that she doesn't know me. When she does, she'll like me.

"Your sweatshirt is cool," I say. "Where did you get it?"

"This? Oh, no…It's just a joke, I got it at the thrift store."

"Oh, okay. So what's the joke?"

"That I'm wearing it."

"Hmm, okay. I think I get it."

Opale places a plate of French toast drowning in syrup on the table and sits across from me. She opens a bottle of sparkling water, grabs an old newspaper folded open to the crossword. I stare at a small damp spot on the wall. Scratch at a bit of dried peanut butter on the table.

I'm sad. I don't have anyone to talk to about it.

I take the risk of being laughed at.

"So that girl, Florence, she's his ex?" I ask.

"Yup."

"Where's she from?"

Opale thinks it over.

"She's a good friend of Maya's brother. They used to be roommates."

She passes the puck to Maya, who's standing by the stove.

"Dave met Florence when they were doing their undergrad in communications," Maya says. "She went on to do a master's, but he opened his own café. She works in advertising now, I think. Some big agency. Project manager or accounts director — something like that."

"And Dave, he's still in love with her?"

"Everyone knows Dave is…" Maya adds butter to the pan.

Opale rushes in to finish the sentence, and they both say it at the same time.

"…not over his ex."

I laugh, but not because it's funny. Maya squints behind her little round glasses.

"I'm surprised he didn't tell you. He talks about her a lot, Florence. Like, all the time, to everybody."

That makes Opale laugh, a squeaky laugh. And it comes back to me like a slap in the face. He did talk about her, yes. At Alice's last party. Right here, in this kitchen. He said it word for word. That he wasn't over his ex. That's why I stalked her, but I thought it was ancient history. That he would have me now, that he wouldn't need her anymore.

I breathe out a long sigh.

"They've been screwing around for a couple of years," Maya says. "She leaves him, then she comes back on and off, when she feels like it, when she gets bored with dating apps. It looked like she was seeing another guy this summer, but he left to live in France."

Maya slides a steaming plate in front of me and goes back to the stove. Opale makes air quotes and says, "She doesn't see herself with Dave, but she doesn't see herself without Dave."

I sigh. "I hate her."

"That makes two of us."

Maya comes back with her plate and a jar of palm oil–free hazelnut spread. She sits beside me and jokes to Opale, "You just hate her because she's kind of dumb."

"No, no. I hate her because she thinks she's so edgy when she just acts exactly like everyone else in the world, and because she has absolutely no sense of humor and absolutely no self-insight and no desire to change," Opale replies.

"True. And she wears two-hundred-dollar jeans."

"Reads graphic novels."

"Thinks Angela Davis is a singer."

"Buys zero-waste kits."

"Only drinks flat whites."

"Only blows film producers."

Opale turns to me with a smile. "You see? We're on your side."

I am oddly flattered. I see a gleam in Opale's eyes. She likes to call people out, find their flaws. She really gets off on it. Maybe it's one of the only ways to bond with her. Hate something as much as she does.

I take a stab at it.

"The kind of girl who likes to look down on you in spite of the fact that she's just sooo basic."

"Ha! Exactly!"

"Her voice is terrible."

"She's always playing the woman-child. There's nothing I hate more. Seriously, deal with your daddy issues."

Yikes. I don't dare to imagine what they say about me when I'm not around. I smile, but I'm feeling a bit hungover after being so bitchy about a perfect stranger. Also feeling a bit bad for having so much fun.

Maya starts to eat her spread right out of the jar. Opale goes back to her crossword. I ask myself why she came to help me yesterday. Surely because I'm the sister of her girlfriend, or rather her not-girlfriend.

"Okay, so wouldn't Alice try to warn me about her?"

Opale shrugs.

"We never thought you'd leave your boyfriend."

Oh, my God, what was I thinking?

"If this goes beyond these walls, I will kill you."

I say it in all seriousness. Wait for a good five seconds before smiling.

Opale stares at me, amazed. It's a look I've never seen from her — I don't hate it.

CELEBRITY WORLD

Seb Hadiba targeted with allegations of sexual assault

This morning YouTuber Seb Hadiba responded to allegations accusing him of using his popularity to gain favors or coerce young girls into sexual relationships. Several of his collaborators have already announced that they have severed their business ties and distanced themselves . . .

Maëla Djeb criticizes Cath Bonenfant in a heated post

Maëla Djeb stated publicly what she thinks of influencer Cath Bonenfant's decision to talk about her buttock injections on Instagram. In a lengthy post on her Facebook page, Maëla explains why she is uncomfortable with Cath's decision to promote the use of surgical intervention . . .

Breakup for Cloé Greene and Liam St-Pierre

Fans of Tellement Cloé and Liam St-Pierre have been aware for a while that Cloé and Liam, new parents of little William, have separated. What has been a rumor up until now was confirmed yesterday by the actor on his Facebook page. In fact, he was responding to a comment from a web user who asked why the lovers' posts . . .

19

I meet Mila at Browz. Huge room, white walls, concrete floor, white counter. Along the sides are little cubicles separated by big white curtains. There are white balloons hanging everywhere and a dozen girls on their phones and drinking bubbly.

Typical. I can't judge, I would be doing the same thing.

I give them Mila's name. I'm handed a glass of sparkling wine, a white bag which I imagine contains white gifts, and they direct me to the back, where Mila is waiting for me, sitting on a white chair, looking deeply bored. She's wearing a knockout outfit — pigtails, a mauvey-blue nylon dress, little white socks and fluorescent yellow sneakers. She looks fabulous.

She stands up when she sees me. Her shoes light up when she walks.

"Awesome."

"Thanks. This is the sporty retro micro-collection by Aimée-Jade Bissonnette for Banana Apparel. I'm wearing their anorak dress. Hot, huh? I wanted to wait for your launch to wear it, but I just couldn't.

Anyway, it's okay, because I've decided I'm an outfit repeater."

She does a little twirl.

"Soon I'll be developing my own exclusive collection. Then I'll document my creative process in a mini web series on my channel."

Okay, I'll admit it. I'm impressed. I don't know anyone who's as determined as she is. Hardworking, too. And she's talented, I have to say.

And I will say it. One day. And in the meantime, I talk about the first thing that comes into my head.

"Did you see the thing about Seb Hadiba? I don't believe it! He's a friend of yours, right?"

Mila's face changes color. Her eyes drop to her chair.

Oops, maybe this isn't small-talk material. She mumbles something about "Yeah, it's crazy," and stares at nothing.

I sit in her silence. My nose in my glass, I'm trying to think of a better topic of conversation when an aesthetician in a white linen top comes to find us. Her name is Debbie. She wants to know which of us is Ellie. I raise my hand.

Pleased, she motions to us to follow her, pulls

aside a white curtain to lead us into a small cubicle that's lit up like an operating room. She shows me to a kind of white padded lounge chair. I place my glass of bubbly on the floor and lie down, wondering what I'm doing there. Mila comes in with two more glasses of champagne. She sits on the chair beside me and tucks one leg under her bottom.

"It's perfect that you're here. I can document the whole procedure in one of my posts. I'll tag you, though. Don't worry."

"What procedure?"

"The lamination."

"The what?"

"It's like a perm, but for your eyebrows. All the brow gurus are obsessed with it right now."

"Okay, but why aren't you trying it?"

"Nah, my eyebrows are already super full, can you just imagine?"

No, in fact I can't imagine. That's my point. But by the time I realize what's happening, Debbie has already begun to briskly clean my brows with makeup remover pads.

"Okay," she says, "I'll explain how this works. We apply the glue, we brush everything up to create some nice fluff, we let it set, we dye, we pluck, and then we finish with a nourishing hybrid treatment. Sound good?"

"A hybrid treatment?"

"To hydrate and protect."

"From?"

"Pollution...the elements. Anything that might weaken your eyebrows."

Ah, well, sure. Eyebrow weakness — the plague everyone is talking about.

While Mila takes big close-ups of my face, I realize that I am lying on a luxury lounge chair about to have my eyebrows permed. Once again she has managed to manipulate me into an uncomfortable situation without me realizing it.

Damn it. I was so preoccupied with plans for the trip that I didn't see it coming.

"Oh!" she says, scrolling through her phone. "Okay, let me tell you about the New Year's Festival!"

She starts talking away about all the steps she's taken over the past three months to convince the VP of marketing at Banana Apparel to send her to New Zealand to produce content for the brand. Tells me how she's contacted a "super well-known" photographer there to take photos of us during the festival and how he was blown away by her mood board. She says she's already reserved youth hostels since the hotels have been booked since October. That she's arranged for media accreditations and the passes are already on their way. That she practically can't sleep at night because she has always dreamed of going there.

She talks and talks, and the champagne starts to do its job.

To go far away. For a long time. The idea starts to bubble up in my head. I want to go right now. I wonder why the airline tickets haven't been bought yet. Count down the days. Think about how Dave might react when he sees me living the good life in New Zealand. He'll be sorry. Of course he'll message me, but I'll already be far away and not in a hurry to come back. Sorry not sorry.

"Can you imagine," Mila says, practically out of breath, "celebrating New Year's on the beach with The Naked and Famous? It'll be the experience of a lifetime. There are so many things I want to see and do. Like absolutely go hiking at Milford Sound or Lake Marian. I'm not sure we'll have the time in five days, but we'll have to tr —"

"Well, we're not going to sit in a plane for thirty hours just to stay for five days! We'll rent a car and wander around. Two weeks or more wouldn't hurt. You only live once!"

"Ha, ha. I'd love that, of course, but we won't have enough money. As it is we'll be eating canned tuna and protein bars to come in on budget…although that won't be much different than what we do here!"

I laugh loudly. Oops, I am officially tipsy, but so is Mila, it would seem. It is wonderfully relaxing to have your brows done by an expert.

It gives me an idea.

"Okay, then if we brought more visibility to the brand, do you think they would be up for increasing the budget? What would we need — two or three thousand dollars? It's small change for them."

"Maybe."

"I can pitch an idea to *Femme* for a magazine article. A three- or four-page feature about our adventures. A behind-the-scenes account of the trip with photos. I would absolutely love to write it, too!"

"Doesn't hurt to try. I'll put you in contact with the VP at Banana."

"Don't worry. I'll make it so they can't say no. As in 'If you want something, don't wait for someone to give it to you. Take it.'"

"Wow, you remember that?"

"Red carpet of the Anti-Bullying Gala? Of course. It was unforgettable."

I laugh. Mila looks at me and smiles affectionately. It warms my little heart. Debbie applies plastic film to my eyebrows "to allow the glue to set." She leaves us alone and promises to return in five minutes. Mila offers me another glass of bubbly, and I lift myself up on my elbows to drink it. She films us with one hand as we clink glasses. With plastic wrap on my forehead and everything, it's going to look kind of ridiculous.

"Don't worry, I'm not going to post it!" she says, putting down her phone.

"Ha, ha...yeah, no...good. Thanks, by the way. I'm really happy you chose me to come on the trip."

"Stop it, it's nothing."

"I owe you one. I have your back, too. You can trust me on that."

I can see that she's happy to hear it, but mostly it's me who feels good all of a sudden. I have a hard time believing that it has come to this, but I mean it.

I like this girl. We have so many things in common. If I hadn't spent so much time trying to be better than her…it took me a long time to realize that the two of us are stronger together. This trip is proof.

"It's funny that you mention that gala," she says softly, "because…that night, Seb — Seb Hadiba, I… we…oh, never mind. Forget it."

"No, if you want to talk about it, talk. I promise, no judgment."

Mila sighs loudly. She looks so serious all of a sudden. I sit back in my chair.

"I don't know how…" she starts nervously, "…okay, so that night, we were flirting. It was cool… then at a some point he pulled me into a corner to kiss me — lots of tongue. I was surprised, but I consented 100 percent. Like, I really wanted this guy to notice me, you know what I mean? I've always loved his videos, I thought they were hilarious. He said all sorts of nice things to me. We talked about some nice projects for our channels. He even wanted to come to New Zealand, pay his own way, everything…I was floating on a little cloud when he took my hand to lead me to the bathroom. I wanted to kiss him, I told myself we would have more privacy, I don't know,

I was just happy to be with him. He pulled me into a stall, locked the door, pulled down his pants and . . . I froze. I didn't want to do it, not like that, anyway. I should have left . . . I said that I didn't want to, but he just kept going. I remember saying that I wanted to take my time, that things were going too fast, but he didn't listen. At the same time, I felt bad that I kissed him and that things had got this far without me doing anything, you know what I mean?"

I nodded. To let her know I did understand, that I was on her side.

"I did what he wanted. Then after a few minutes, it was over. He didn't even warn me before he . . . After, he left saying that it would stay 'between us.' And then he winked at me. I was crying, and that didn't even bother him. I felt like such a loser."

"You're not a loser."

"That night, he posted his first official couple selfie with Jordanne Jacques. Seems they'd already been going together for two weeks."

"Agh, you're kidding!"

"I feel sick when I think about it. And then I started to read about the accusations against him, and looking back I realized he did the same thing to girls who weren't even sixteen! So that's it, I don't know why I've told you so much, but…do you think I should speak out against him, too? Will people believe me?"

I wish I could put my arms around her, tell her that I don't think I could say no either. I would like to tell her something to make her feel less alone. To be as vulnerable in return. To let her know I'm not with Sam anymore. That I broke his heart over a guy who didn't even matter. To share that, expose myself.

"I believe you. So if you think that reporting him will —"

But Debbie, my brow guru, cuts me short by sailing through the curtains. Mila immediately goes back to looking like a girl who's all business. The contrast is funny. I feel like I've seen inside her, seen the real her. While Debbie colors my eye mustaches, I come down a bit from the bubbly. Kind of drowsy, muzzy-headed, my mouth full of cotton.

After about a century, she hands me a mirror and says, "There you go, my beauty. The results will be visible for about six to eight weeks."

I look in the mirror while Mila films my reaction.

Holy shit, I have two caterpillars crawling across my forehead.

SELF-CONFIDENCE

I get jealous. Always of other women. Never men. I've learned not to compare myself to men.

But women? I'm always judging them. It's stronger than me, like an automatic reflex, and I don't even realize I'm doing it. The ones with big noses, the ones who put on weight, the ones who lose it. Girls who stick their tongues out in photos. Or the ones who look too eager to please. The ones whose Botox is completely obvious. Who wear too much eyeliner. Whose lips are too swollen. Who have breasts that look fake. Who strike a pose.

As if those standards of beauty aren't all fake to start with — the idea that you can and should look a certain way. But I don't care. I like to find fault anyway. Because I've learned that you have to meet certain standards even if you don't really want to. You have to seduce without really trying. Wear makeup, but look totally natural. Be thin, but don't obsess about food. Look desirable, but not like a slut. Happy, but not dumb. Vulnerable, but not broken.

I win by putting them down. By judging my own worth against theirs. If they're too slutty or ugly, I win.

If they're too beautiful or smart, I lose. Too bad.

I was made to be this way. Insecure about never being good enough. A body to be conquered. Pitting myself against everyone else. Measured by what I want, by my actions. Yet the idea of letting myself want is foreign to me. I suck in my stomach and smile. I have many rivals, but very few friends.

And then one day the accusations will flow into my own feed by the hundreds. Rivers, torrents of women who I've envied, judged, laughed at. My adversaries. I can hear them say, "Me too." Talking about how their bodies have been trampled, their hearts. How they've been broken.

And I feel ridiculous. Ridiculous for thinking we were any different. That we were in competition with each other. For having believed them when they told me there was a right way to be a woman.

I'm ashamed that I forgot we were sisters.

20

I leave Browz around 3:00 p.m., a little groggy after all the sparkling wine. I order a taxi. I'm starving, I've eaten nothing since the French toast with Alice's roommates, so I stop at the convenience store before going back to the apartment. I realize there is absolutely nothing there to buy that I can eat, but I'm so hungry that my judgment is impaired, so I buy a small gâteau Maurice. The kind of treat I would dream about when I was little, but that my mother always refused to buy. The only treats that dared enter our house were carefully hidden and then distributed with strict parental supervision. Even as an adult, I never gave myself permission to eat this kind of thing. Too many calories, too much sugar, too much guilt.

I grab a snack cake off the shelf, hesitate. I think about my launch in ten days…

I take it anyway, realize that no one is stopping me, that I have the right. I have the right! I feel like a real badass, free. While I'm at it, I buy a lottery ticket at the cash. That's another thing I never do. I'm tickled to bits by this, imagine myself traveling to New Zealand on an unlimited budget.

I pay, leave the shop and smile as I walk home. My boots sink into the little frozen puddles that crackle beneath my feet. The cold air whips up my spirits. The sun is shining, I feel good. It's weird, given that I'm sad. Drinking bubbly in the afternoon, making free choices, listening to myself. Being myself, just me, not the girl I'm supposed to be. Is that even possible?

I go back to the apartment with my lottery ticket and my little cake. Happy. Get tangled up in the Home Sweet Home carpet at the door, stumble over a pair of shoes and crash into the wall. Oopsie.

From the kitchen, Sam looks at me, puzzled.

"You okay?"

I make an effort to look normal, even though I'm feeling a bit confused.

"First of all, I just slipped."

He walks toward me, stares at me in a weird way. I put a hand in front of my forehead.

"Oh, that," I say. "It's because I had a lamation. A lamnation. I had my eyebrows laminated. Ta-dah!"

I remove my hand to reveal my face.

Sam frowns, looks at the time.

"Have you been drinking?"

"Yes, some sparkling wine. They just kept pouring!"

"Who did?"

"The brow gurus."

I burst out laughing, but Sam does not. He almost looks serious.

"What are you doing, Élisabeth?" he says in an even voice.

"Nothing, Samuel. I'm not doing a thing. I was with Mila, we drank some bubbly, and now I have full eyebrows. That's all."

I gesture for him to step aside so I can get by, but he doesn't budge.

"I'm worried about you," he says sadly.

"Stop it. That's enough."

"I think you're about to ruin something important."

"What are you talking about? I'm not ruining anything. Let me through."

He crosses his arms and looks at the piece of cake in my hand. I roll my eyes.

"You are such a cliché," I say. "Jesus, you're such a drag. And so absolutely predictable."

"No, listen, things aren't right. You're taking a big risk right now."

I don't know what to say. I just stand there in the

hall, in my little socks, with my little piece of cake, my big lottery ticket. The air is heavy, and so are my eyelids. I'm being bullied.

"There's nothing wrong!" I say. "You can stop worrying, because I am just fine! I've got some interesting projects and I'm finally getting to be more like myself, don't you get it? And I like it! Okay? I am fine!"

"If you say so..."

Sam puts his hands behind his neck and cradles his head in his forearms. He looks at me, his eyes full of sarcasm, even contempt.

It makes me mad. I grit my teeth.

"I have just landed a trip to New Zealand," I burst out. "Hello! I am capable of living without you, I am capable of being successful! I know it must be difficult to believe, but the world does not just revolve around Samuel Vanasse. I exist without you! And you know what? I think I like the person I am when you aren't there."

I'm gloating, and it makes me feel great to say this to his face. I could keep this up for hours. I'm ready, I'm strong, I can defend myself.

Sam, on the other hand, loses patience.

"If you love yourself that much," he snaps, his eyes

big, his arms raised to the sky, "that girl that you are without me? Why have you been retouching all your photos since we broke up?"

I never told him about retouching my photos, my little secret with Face Optimizer. He figured it out himself. Shit.

I start to stutter, dissolve into a little puddle — a small, confused puddle.

"Why are you just posting stuff that we filmed months ago?" Sam continues smugly.

"I...no..."

"This isn't like you, Ellie! That girl I see on your Insta, the one who's so successful with all her projects. I'm sorry, but you haven't been that girl for some time. That's not the girl standing in front of me right now, eating junk food and drunk at three o'clock in the afternoon. No matter how much you want it to be true, your 'real' self is not what people love. That's not the girl who's getting the big contracts. You're not that person anymore. You may not realize it at the moment, but you are running straight into a big wall and you are about to crash. I'm sorry to be the one to tell you, but you can't carry on like this for much longer."

I swallow. Struggle to catch my breath.

Sam bites his lip. He's said too much. He went too far, and he's sorry already.

But I know he's right. His words take root in my chest.

It's too much.

"Go fuck yourself," I say.

"I'm sorry..."

"FUCK OFF."

"I'm sorry," he says, lowering his head. "I'm trying to help you...I'm starting to feel like I'm losing the person I love more than anyone in the world. You're so different, it's —"

"Just drop it, okay?"

He leans against the wall, sinks down to the floor, puts his head between his knees.

I make my way around him.

"Tell me how to help you, please. I love you, Ellie, I know that much."

Infuriated, I walk away to the kitchen, turn around and retrace my steps.

"Okay, I've had enough. I'm going to go and live at Alice's."

"Go ahead then. Do that!"

I turn away again, slam the door, shut myself in my

room. I cry for a long time, rolled up in a little ball on the cold floor. I wait. I scratch my lottery ticket praying for rescue, a big win, a new story. To reinvent myself.

My nail comes away black. It's a losing ticket.

I rip it into pieces, make a little pile and blow on it. The confetti of misfortune. I watch the pieces scatter on the ground around me, pathetic.

My stomach grumbles. I'm hungry. Why am I even here?

I take my little cake. The plastic crinkles in my hand. I squish it a little bit. Inside is a heavy, moist cake protected in its plastic bubble of air. It must be good. With my fingertips I press gently, and the chocolate icing melts a bit against the plastic. I read the label — 400 calories. That's two cups of cooked rice. Or four slices of multigrain bread. Two avocados. Five mini chocolate bars. A block of tofu.

Four hundred calories.

I close my eyes. Think about Florence Marquis, how her jeans floated around her waist. About Dave when he looks at her. Her artsy style that is cool, mysterious. Perfect.

I'm not on her level. It's practically a joke. I'm a turd next to a flower.

I wait. There is nothing left to do with myself, with my sadness that swells, flows, spreads. I am an Olympic pool of ugliness. I swim in this despair with no limit. An insignificant tragedy. The story of a girl who wanted to be herself, but who forgot that no one loves her. Just me.

I let myself sink down until my feet touch the bottom. I stay there a moment, waiting, getting bored. I miss the air, my hands reach up to the surface. I get my phone, open Instagram, scroll through my feed, suck in the photos, breathe them in one by one. Selena St-Aubin, Becky Robins, Mila Mongeau, Audrey Sylvestre, Samantha Larochelle, Jordanne Jacques, Sarah Rondeau.

I emerge. It's beautiful and inspiring. These girls — these girls deserve to be alive.

I calculate. Ten days until my launch, 240 hours, 14,400 minutes.

I fall down, and I get back up again. It goes without saying...

Goes without saying.

#HAPPYLIVING

– Breathing
– Juicing
– Gratitude
– Getting up before the sun
– Getting your nine hours of sleep
– Journaling
– Slow living
– Probiotics
– Lagom
– Self-love
– Crystals
– Learning forgiveness
– Breathing
– Omega-3
– Yoga
– Letting go
– Small candles
– Hygge
– Making the most of things
– Breaking free
– The importance of a morning routine
– Developing self-confidence

- Unplugging
- Being able to laugh about it
- Thermal spas
- Vitamin D
- Being mindful
- Learning to forgive YOU
- The sun
- Reconnecting
- Art therapy
- Apple cider vinegar
- Breathing through the nose
- Therapy pets
- The importance of nature
- Smiling
- CBD
- The Four Agreements
- Communicating
- Essential oils
- Slowing down
- Moving
- Self-care
- Empower yourself
- Light therapy
- Herbal tea

- Orgasm
- Astrology
- The plant-based diet
- Learning to love yourself
- Believing in yourself
- Sandalwood
- Detox
- Marine collagen
- Adult coloring books
- Massage therapy
- Acupuncture
- Burning sage
- Being a good person
- Netflix
- Mastering the art of not giving a fuck
- Aligning your chakras
- Hypnosis
- Decluttering
- Walking barefoot in the grass
- Travel
- Breathing, but well
- Becoming your own best friend
- Visualizing
- Jack Johnson on a loop

- Believing in it harder
- The importance of the lunar cycle
- The power of intention
- Interpreting your dreams
- Reiki
- Positive waves
- Giving
- Breathing through the belly
- Learning to say no
- JOMO
- De-dramatizing
- Always breathing better
- Planning a staycation
- Breathing

Email sent by Souad Faez, Thursday, November 15, 2:42 p.m.

Subject: New Year's Festival partnership

Hello Ellie,

First, let me say that I'm a big fan of your recipe for sweet potato brownies! So good! I replace the coconut sugar with applesauce, add a cup of sour cream, a touch of vanilla, and voilà, it's excellent!

That being said, I have received your proposal concerning *Femme* magazine. Are you available to discuss?

Souad Faez

VP Marketing, Innovation, Competitive Positioning and Strategic Development

Banana Apparel

Email sent by Estelle Bourdon, Monday, November 19, 5:27 p.m.

Subject: Back soon . . .

Hello my dear . . . Everything is fine . . . Our flight home is Wednesday at 8:05 p.m. . . . Will take a cab home . . .

Can't wait for your launch ;-) ;-) ;-) ;-)

Have you talked to your father . . .??? Hasta pronto and kisses to Sam!!!

Sent from my iTab

21

I kept my word to Sam and moved in with my sister. Today it's been one week since I left with three suitcases, a backpack and two fat eyebrows. One week since I promised Alice I would clean her apartment in exchange for her hospitality for an undetermined length of time. She couldn't say no. I'm her sister.

I spent the first few days wandering between the refrigerator and the couch. Collecting minutes of silence. Baking muffins and pretending that I wasn't going to eat them. Reading uplifting things like "99 things to do after a breakup" — thank you, Google — then finding that it's quite a big to-do list for a girl who has trouble finding the motivation to brush her teeth. I focus on numbers 32 and 58, which are Cry and Advance my career. The results are mixed.

Living with Alice, Opale (her roommate slash girlfriend slash not girlfriend) and Maya, the other roommate I never run into is, well...weird. I had to get used to a lot of things.

First of all, it is always 18 degrees in here. The apartment is so old that the cold air sneaks in through every crack, but there's no question of turning up the heat because then Alice gives you her death stare. I dress accordingly. Many layers. I look like a marshmallow. The only problem is that the tip of my nose is always frozen.

Second thing is that I have no privacy here. Whenever I spend a bit of time in the apartment, Opale is underfoot. She sits near me and pretends to read books with long-winded titles. Like, yesterday it was *Gender Trouble: Feminism and the Subversion of Identity*.

Okay, so I know this sounds like I'm exaggerating, but it's like she's spying on me.

Third thing, and worst of all, is the fridge. Let's just say there are leftovers in there that have been around since the not-so-fine days of Sean Paul. It's getting busy inside that Tupperware.

It gets to the point that when I get back from the grocery store, I decide to clean up. Decide to deal with those refrigerator issues, bring it up to certified quality. There is no way I'm going to put my organic vegetables between an open tin of ham flakes and an old hot dog bun wrapped in a tea towel.

The timing is good anyway, because I've decided that today is the first day of the rest of my life. I dropped by the apartment to pick up the rest of my things while Sam was out, and now I am taking control of my new surroundings.

I start at 9:00 a.m. I am in the middle of emptying the condiment shelf when Opale, who is sitting at the kitchen table, lifts her nose out of her book, looks at me and says with a faintly bored look, "You don't have to do that."

I want to tell her that at this point, housecleaning is not a luxury. But because she's had the infinite kindness to lend me her room and sleep in Alice's, I try not to antagonize her.

"No, I want to!"

"Really?"

"Honestly, if you asked me whether I would choose to have an orgasm, say, or the satisfaction of opening a perfectly tidied-organized-cleaned fridge, I would choose the fridge. No contest."

"Sounds like fun, being hetero."

"Well, this old mustard has a best before date of May 2016."

"Then knock yourself out."

I scrub, label, wipe, scrape and toss. Crumbs, a pool of syrup. Some sketchy-looking juice. I forget about everything else. And the more I clean, the better I feel.

I've let myself get depressed lately, wasn't paying attention to my own mindset, but that's all over. Because I'm not going to accomplish anything by feeling sorry for myself. Let alone get Dave to love me more than his ex.

No, starting from now, it's good vibes only.

"Okay," I say brightly as I empty the fridge drawers, "for your information, this drawer is perfect for keeping food that you want to retain its moisture, such as many fruits like grapes, peaches, apples. It is not optimal for storing beer, and you should..."

While I'm talking, Opale gets up and starts to rummage through my grocery bags. Unpacks my things. I don't know exactly why, but I find it intrusive. I want to tell her to stop. Immediately.

"You don't want to go in with us on our joint grocery shopping?"

The girls do a big shop every Thursday. They buy random stuff according to what they feel like — macaroni in a box, chicken pâté, linguine with rosé sauce. I don't know how they can eat like that. Eat whatever they want whenever they want. Because if I'm not trying to lose weight, I'm gaining it.

"You just write any special requests here," Opale says. "We'll keep track."

She points at a Post-it on the fridge, where Alice has written "orange juice with pulp" and "Cap'n Crunch cereal!!!" then gives me a challenging look. She waits for my reaction like she's testing me.

"Yes, no, well…" I sputter. "It's just simpler if I buy my own groceries."

The truth is that I started the Becky Robins Fat Burning Challenge a couple of days ago. Rebecca Robinson, her real name, is an American who *Forces* magazine named one of the Top 30 under 30. Her "10-minute six-pack" workout has received 40 million views on YouTube. She sells cookbooks, sugar-free chocolate chips, protein bars. She even has her own app. I paid seventy-five bucks US for a one-month meal plan and workouts. The first two weeks are a bit intense. You have to limit yourself to a certain number of calories a day, and there is a list of permitted foods.

I know it's stupid, that diets don't work… I've said as much hundreds of times to my own followers that I'm "against" them. Except I have no other option right now — the goal of losing seven pounds in seven days is the only thing that gets me up in the morning.

And the last thing I need is Opale sticking her big full-of-judgment nose in my business.

She points to a package that I brought into the apartment.

"What is that, 'a way to achieve remarkable beauty through the amazing power of grapefruit'?"

She laughs. My shoulders stiffen.

"Those are gummy vitamins," I say, irritated. "They're like jujubes, but they contain good things for the skin. It's a contract. I have to do a post on them."

She takes the bottle and looks at it with disdain.

"Wow. They write 'beauty' on a package of jujubes and people will buy this! Better they should pay you, a girl with body-image issues, to talk to other girls with body-image issues. This is truly a fascinating business."

"Thanks, Opale, but I think the reality is a little more nuanced than that."

"Hardly."

"Don't worry, I'll let you know when they invent 'optimism' jujubes."

"They already have. It's called cannabis."

"Oh, sure."

I think she's starting to sense my annoyance.

"Did I offend you?"

"Bah...no, but sometimes I think you leap to conclusions that are simplistic."

"You're simplistic!"

What? I freeze. That was uncalled for.

"Don't make that face, Ellie. It's a joke. A game. Like if you say that the book you're reading is mediocre, and I say..."

"...that it's excellent even if you haven't read it."

"No! I say, 'You're mediocre!'"

"Oh. Okay. Hilarious."

"Okay, whatever. You'll get the hang of it."

After thoroughly examining the contents of my bags, she leans one buttock on the table, narrows her eyes, crosses her arms and stares at me. I feel like taking one of the three jars of Dijon mustard on the counter and smashing it to the ground. Watch it hit the floor, explode into pieces. Turn into a sharp, slimy puddle.

What has gotten into me? It's weird.

"Can I help you with anything else?" I ask, annoyed.

"I just wanted to say, I...I am sorry about your father. It's sad."

I'm stunned. Opale talking to me about my father. It catches me off guard.

"Alice introduced me to him yesterday. He's a fascinating person. I can't believe he really taught literature in Paris? He's so eloquent, so committed! Is it true he campaigned for watershed conservation back in the nineties? It's amazing how much he's done in his life. I would have liked to get to know him. To have known him for a long time, I mean…"

She adds, "It must have been amazing growing up with a father like that!"

"Yeah. It was…yeah."

She sits back down, picks up her book. "I know it's none of my business, but I think you should go and see him…Alice says he talks about you a lot."

I nod and go back to cleaning out the fridge. I try to concentrate. To think about something else, but my eyes fill with tears. I cry with my head in the fruit drawer. I cry as I scrub away at little spots of ketchup. I don't want Opale to see me. Not like this. It's like that's all I've been doing for the past week — crying.

Tomorrow. Tomorrow is going to be the first day of the rest of my life. Tomorrow it's good vibes only.

Tomorrow, I'm going to get it together.

PAPA

Valentine's Day. I am nine years old. My father comes home from work late. We've already eaten supper, we've been waiting for him before we eat dessert. Lying on my stomach on the floor of my room, I'm making bracelets. He comes in, and I just see his feet. A clumsy giant, he knocks over a tube of pink beads. They fall out onto the floor. I scoop up the rest — my plastic diamonds, my shiny little marbles, my golden clasps. I surround them with my arms like a fortress.

He's talking loudly, his big serious voice filling the room. He's mad because I failed my math test. Fifty-four percent. I'm supposed to put my things away, go to bed. I'm not allowed to come out of my room until tomorrow morning.

My mother has made a cake. A tiramisu in a heart-shaped mold, I couldn't wait to eat it. I can hear them — Alice and my parents — celebrating the holiday of love. Celebrating without me.

The next morning, in my lunch box, there's a piece of cake in a plastic container. A little shapeless pile of chocolate and creamy pastry. Crushed.

22

I listened to Opale and called my father to tell him I would come by to see him after lunch. I got there at 2:00 p.m. He had set the table — napkins, place mats, little forks. He'd defrosted a cherry tart. He was waiting for me.

I didn't know what to do. His body was emaciated and gray. His eyes glassy. There were pieces of medical equipment everywhere, piles of moving boxes.

Death as interior decorator.

He asked how I was doing, congratulated me again on my book, on my upcoming marriage. Said he was happy to see me, his eyes filled with a new tenderness.

I ate in silence, a lump in my throat, did the dishes, unable to say anything, to talk about the situation.

Until we were in the living room. I pointed to the game of Scrabble on the coffee table and said the only thing that would come out of my mouth.

"Ha! Remember how we used to play after dinner at the cottage?"

My father smiles, nods his head.

"You always won," I add. "You are a very poor winner, by the way."

"If you must know, I am an even worse loser."

"I don't doubt it for two seconds."

That makes him laugh, and he starts to cough. Nonstop. Sitting in his armchair, out of breath. He closes his eyes for a long time, as if he's going to fall asleep. I leave him be for a moment. I walk over to the boxes. I recognize objects from my childhood — a table clock, a porcelain horse, a painting of the sunset at the cottage.

I stop in front of a frame leaning against the wall. It's a photo of me taken in daycare — a professional photo with a backdrop, adequate lighting. I'm wearing an outfit chosen by my mother.

I look at the child I used to be. I have no memory of her, I don't know her. I look into her eyes for traces of the person I've turned into. I find none.

I put down the frame, turn around to see the small icy blue eyes of my father gazing at me.

"Will you give me a hug?" he asks.

I freeze. I can't remember the last time we embraced or even touched. The idea feels strange. Too strange.

"Or just hold my hand. Time is running out, my big girl, I'm going to —"

"I know, Papa."

His eyes are as blue as water, a teardrop as big as a lake. I kneel down beside him, hold out my hand. He takes it, holds it awkwardly, crushes my fingers, then closes his eyes. His skin against mine feels like clammy, icy cold plastic wrap.

I stop breathing. I feel uncomfortable, but I make an effort not to move, to stay. Just stay.

He finally lets go of my hand.

"I love you," my father says.

It shakes me. I tense up, resist. I am very aware that time is of the essence, that I need to say something back. To say I love him, too, would be too simple. The cherry tart, the napkins, I love you, too, and then we wouldn't have to say any more. Everything would be forgotten, everything forgiven.

I make the sounds in my mouth — I-love-you. I push them to the edge of my lips, but I can't make them come out.

In a panic, I say, "I'm so sorry, Papa, that I didn't come before this. I...it's complicated for me."

He looks at me solemnly, and what he says is a

question and a statement at the same time. "I haven't always been kind to you."

I nod, unable to speak. He sinks his chin into his neck a bit. He's serious, thinking.

"It's true that I was a demanding father. Strict but fair. I did it to teach you to excel. I gave you the tools for life — real life. And look at the beautiful strong woman you have become, my coco-pomme. I succeeded."

His eyes are filled with pride.

"I succeeded," he says again.

I lower my head, swallow the words that are trying to come out, decide to let this moment pass. What difference would it make now anyway?

"I'm sure that you did your best, Papa. I'll come back on Saturday. We'll play Scrabble."

He smiles.

"But don't think you're going to beat your old man just because he's sick."

He winks at me. I give him a kiss on the cheek.

"And don't you think I'm going to let you win, just because you're sick."

David Lanctôt has sent you a message

D: Really sorry about the other night. Xx

23

"Oh, geez! Dave just wrote me."

I drop my phone on the kitchen table. Opale puts her fat book down next to her plate of General Tao tofu and her fork goes flying and falls to the floor. Alice picks it up and folds down the top of her laptop.

"Ooh! What does he say?"

"He says he's sorry for the other night. With two kisses."

"Hmmm. Sounds like Daddy wants some sugar!"

"What?"

Alice raises her eyebrows and makes little kissy sounds with her lips.

"He wants you to ride his baloney pony. Of course."

I roll my eyes.

"How old are you, Al — twelve or seventy-two? And what are you talking about, anyway? He's apologizing, that's all."

I start to type a reply to Dave.

"It's none of my business," Opale says, "but I haven't seen Florence at the café for at least a week. Maybe they're already finished. I mean re-re-re-finished. I've lost track."

Alice looks at me and makes penis-in-vagina gestures with her fingers.

I groan and bury my face in my hands.

"Alice, you're being infantile. Besides, it doesn't mean anything. She's away for the weekend with her friends."

"Stalker!" she says, mocking.

"Research and development," I clarify, raising a finger in the air.

"What are you going to do?" Opale asks.

"I've already replied that I said what I had to say, and that I've moved on, which is a big fat lie, I realize, but then, if he's single, that changes everything, doesn't it?"

A shiver of excitement goes through me and stirs my little heart.

My phone vibrates. A new message from Dave. Alice rushes to grab it before me.

She reads it in a loud voice: "'I didn't mean to hurt you.' Oh, come on! We're going to need more than that before we forgive and forget, my little friend."

"My little friend?"

She widens her eyes, sighs and starts to type. I try to take back my phone, but she turns, taps away and presses Send.

"Alice Bourdon-Marois, NO! Don't do that! What did you write?"

I grab the phone out of her hands and read her reply: "It is what it is. Bye!"

"But that's way too boring!"

"Ellie, you are not just going to crawl your way back into his bed."

"No, of course not! But...you're getting too worked up about it. He doesn't even know I've left my boyfriend. Maybe he would never have got back together with his ex. I mean, can we really hold it against him?"

"Stop it. This guy knows very well what he's doing."

She gets up, gets a bottle of vodka out of the freezer, a carton of orange juice from the fridge and some glasses.

"It's time for strong measures."

"What do you mean, he knows what he's doing?"

"Vodka and orange?"

I do the math in my head. About a hundred calories for a small glass. If I skip my pasta with lentils and kale pesto for dinner, I should be good to hang around with them for a bit. And get more information about Dave.

"Okay, but skip the orange juice."

"Wild."

At any rate, things are going well. Five days since I started the Becky Robins challenge, and the weight is falling off like the glaciers of Greenland.

I look at Alice.

"So, about Dave?"

"So, you're not the first person he's done this to."

"Huh? Okay, explain."

"I've heard he does this a lot with girls. Maya told me stories after your French toast breakfast...She felt bad for you, said if she'd known she would have warned you."

Opale stirs her vodka with her fork.

"I know that it happened to Aude, an old employee at the café. She fell head over heels in love with Dave. They would often take their break together in the little office at the back. Long story short, she had a boyfriend, who she left. I think she had ideas, too, because not long after that, Dave went on a trip to Maine with Florence to give their relationship another chance, and we saw no more of the lovely Aude. She didn't even come back to pick up her things. Her hat and her shoes are still in the back."

"That could just be a coincidence."

That's what I want to believe anyway. I don't know what to think anymore. Except for one thing. To find out I'm not the first or only one that he's taken into his little office? That stings.

"You could say it's his specialty," Opale says. "Spotting and seducing girls who are unhappy in their relationships."

Alice thinks about this. "It's true that I've never seen him be interested in a single girl. Then I remember that at one time we tried hard to snag him for ourselves, ha, ha. Remember the shawarma evening?"

Opale laughs, too. "The dying days of my bisexuality, God bless them." She empties her glass. "No, the more I think about it, the more he's a hero deep down, Dave. He gives girls who are bored with their partners the courage to leave."

I sigh, and think that doesn't really describe my situation. I turn to my sister.

"Okay, so what about Maya's other stories?"

"I should text her so she can come and spend the evening! I think I can count on one hand the number of times she's slept here since she started dating Jeff."

"Your prof at the university?"

Opale looks like she couldn't care less.

"That little egomaniac has a bungalow in Old Longueuil. We can't compete with that."

"It's no reason to forget us," says Alice.

"What do you want? She's in love with his dog... Pecan."

"Ugh, why do people become so fucking boring as soon as they pair up?"

My cell vibrates. This time it's Opale who grabs it.

"He replied with three little dots," she says, appalled. "Are you kidding me, dude?"

She shakes her head vigorously.

"Answer him with a question mark. If he wants punctuation, we'll give him punctuation."

"Okay, girls, stop it!"

I squirm in my chair. If it was Alice who had my phone, I would have no shame in leaping on her, snatching it from her hand and giving her a noogie, but I don't dare do that to Opale.

"He's in the middle of writing...okay, here it is, he's replied: 'I feel bad.' Dave, listen, buddy, deal with it."

Draining her glass, Alice says, "Send him three

little dots right back. If that's how he wants to play, so be it."

"Ten-four, mon général!"

Another vibration. It is torture watching them.

"He just wrote, 'Are you OK?' Good, finally he's paying a bit of attention to Ellie's emotions here. Hey, admit that it has been a long time since he's responded this quickly to your messages like this."

"I admit it."

Opale replies to Dave while Alice fills her glass.

"Okay, so there's the proof!" Alice says. "That's the kind of guy he is."

"What kind of guy?" I ask.

"The kind who makes you feel like the most special person in the world, but who loses interest the second you're on the hook, and then perks up again as soon as you start to move on."

"No, no. Not Dave."

Alice puts her finger in front of her mouth to shush me, as though I'm being a bit naive. Opale snaps her fingers and start to sing.

"Two, three, four: *'Oh, thunder only happens when it's raining…'*"

My sister joins in. Together they're singing their

heads off, air guitar and everything.

I listen to them and feel like the heroine of a musical comedy.

"Players only love you when they're playing..."

"Too many karaoke nights, girls," I say. "Way too many."

While they sing, I take the opportunity to grab my phone to read what Opale wrote back in my place. "All good, don't worry."

Ugh. It's super stupid. He's not going to reply to that, obviously.

They keep singing, and there's a new vibration. A new message.

"He answered back! He said, 'OK.'"

It's disappointing. Alice laughs.

"It's Fleetwood Mac!"

"What? No, it's Dave."

"I meant the song."

"Oh, no, I meant his message. Dave, he just said, 'OK.'

"Oh. Stupid."

I shrug.

"What should I do?"

They both reply at the same time.

"Do nothing!"

"Let him off the leash," Opale says. "That's what works with him."

"Let him run," Alice adds. "And then we'll get out the karaoke machine."

"Nooooo, not tonight. I've had it with that."

I don't know how we got to this point, but Alice and Opale have sung just about every major hit by Celine Dion. Smoked a joint. Ate grilled cheese sandwiches with strawberry jam. Sung again.

I gave in and got up on the coffee-table stage to perform "I'm Alive." I even put out a post and you can see that I'm a little tipsy, I admit it. It's not the kind of content I normally share, except I know who will see it. Dave. He watches them all to the end. I wanted him to see me like this. Free, funny, liberated. Far from the uptight and awkward girl he saw at the party the other night.

I come back from the kitchen with a glass of water and plunk myself down beside Alice on my faithful speckled companion. I'm already regretting the alcohol. I hope this doesn't pull me out of my good mindset. My launch is in three days.

I look at my cell.

"You have a serious phone addiction," my sister says.

She takes my phone and tucks it between the couch cushions. Opale sits on my other side. We're sweaty, a bit drunk, a little stinky, braless in our big wool sweaters, but I don't give a shit. I feel good, sandwiched between my two new roommates. The end of my nose isn't cold anymore.

"I wanted to see if he wrote," I say sluggishly to my sister. "I know, I'm pathetic. But I think I'm in love with him."

"Okay, I'm going to tell you something important. Are you ready?"

"Go ahead."

"Love is overrated."

"Maybe. I still think that Dave is the one for me."

Alice pats me gently on the elbow.

"This guy just wants to sleep with you every now and then when the 'woman of his life' dumps him," Opale says. "Seems to me that's obvious. You need to face reality and stop being that poor girl who is so in love with love."

"Okay."

"That's my opinion."

I look at her in amazement, as her legendary bitchiness makes a comeback. I'd almost forgotten this side of her personality.

"That's a bit rude," my sister hurries to add, "but I think what you mean to say, Op, is that Dave probably doesn't see things the way Ellie thinks —"

"No, I mean that I'm fed up with seeing adult women like your sister still waiting for Prince Charming. It's pathetic —"

"Maybe she's not like you, Opale," Alice interrupts, "but that's no reason to be so condescending, okay? I think that sometimes it would do you good to show a little love. It's called empathy..."

"Ah, yes, funny that you're the one who said love was overrated, eh, Alice?" Opale says, getting up from the couch. "I'm sorry, Ellie, this has nothing to do with you. I spoke without thinking."

"No problem."

"Good night."

Pissed off, my sister replies, "Yeah, that's right, good night!"

Opale leaves and shuts herself in her room. There's silence.

"It's not my business," I say, "but I think you hurt your girlfriend's feelings."

"How?"

"When you said that love was overrated."

"Whatever! She knows what I think. And she's not my girlfriend."

"Alice, you 'make love,' you live together, you have plans for the future, you even introduced her to Papa. What does it mean to be a couple if not all that?"

I can see she's upset.

"It means promising things that I can't promise…"

"Hmmm. I think I understand."

"Really?"

"No, but I'm trying. I'm trying hard, Al."

"Asshole."

"You're an asshole. And you smell like armpit."

"I can see your nose boogers."

"At least I don't eat them."

"I've never eaten my boogers!"

"Alice, we both know that isn't true."

"No, I stick them underneath my bed!"

"Agh, that's even worse!"

She yawns, rubs her eyes, says in a little voice, "So…I'm going to bed."

"Okay…I'm here if you want to talk."

"Hmmm. Thanks."

"Don't stick your boogers under your bed."

She drags her feet to her room. I realize that I've lost my room for the night — or rather, Opale's room.

A little sad, I lie down on my old faithful sofa. Stretch out my arm to find my phone in the cushions to see what time it is.

Surprise, surprise, Dave has written me.

"It would be cool to see you soon! If you're tempted, it means you've forgiven me. xxx."

If I'd seen his message fifteen minutes ago, I would have been super happy. Now it's not clear. One thing's for sure, I haven't stopped thinking about him for a single minute. If only he knew how obsessed I am with him.

Alice comes back into the living room.

"What are you doing? Come to sleep!"

I leave my phone in the sofa.

"Oh, yay, a real bed. Thank you, thank you!"

And I trot after her to her room — a bit happy, a bit sad and absolutely starving.

FOOD PORN

When I was younger, some evenings before I fell asleep, I would close my eyes and imagine eating forbidden things. A maple-glazed doughnut, a slice of white bread, chocolate chip cookies...I wanted to stuff myself with the very idea of certain foods, recreate their texture, their taste. Finally, a pleasure without limits. Filling my head so I would never again want to eat with my mouth. I told myself it would make the days easier to bear. That it would help me get through my lunches of a sandwich with brown bread, vegetable pâté, mustard, spinach and no-fat yogurt.

I made myself a lot of little imaginary feasts like that. Until the night I stopped cold when I started to worry that my brain was registering fictitious calories. Psychosomatic calories. Even thinking about food became forbidden.

It's amazing how many doctors, psychologists and nutritionists I visited, when the only thing they accomplished was to help me develop a true obsession with food. A splendid obsession. Whether I eat, when I eat, why I eat. I completely assimilated the idea that by depriving myself, by starving myself, I would become an exemplary person. And in the meantime, I became enemy number one. Under surveillance. I mistrusted my own desires, my own wishes.

Everything becomes bearable when I try to lose weight. When I embark on a new program, a meal plan, a challenge, a "lifestyle." The promise that this will put everything in order, change everything. It gets me going. The idea that one day I will get there, one day I will have done enough.

In the meantime, everything is tolerable, because it is all still achievable. I hold my destiny in my own hands. One renunciation at a time, I become master of my own desires. I starve myself. I deny myself.

Look at how good I am at forgetting myself. Making myself not want anything. Not need anything. Look how small I am becoming.

4,412 Likes

ellie_quinoa_forever Four reasons why I'm feeling really good lately:

• I started taking Beauty gummy vitamins from **@activenaturals** which are packed with ingredients that help keep my skin healthy and hair shiny.

• They are sugar-free, without artificial flavors or dyes.

• I am proud to support a company that is certified ECO Smart.

• I love their amazing grapefruit flavor!

All Active Naturals products are available on the **@selfcaredotca** website, which makes them super easy to order! 15% off with code ELLIE15 **#ad #selfcare #health #ecofriendly**

See all 29 comments

mila.mongeau I feel you girl!!!

sam_van The best.

bella_lifestyle You're hot!

martinayolo I love these vitamins, can't do without them!

sophialabanana So beautiful.

lea.mondoux @ellie_quinoa_forever Certified "ECO Smart" is just big greenwashing. I'll send you the info in a private message. Happy to discuss it if you want.

estellamurphy What a beautiful smile.

seb_123 Whore.

olivia_delisle I really think you have changed without really changing. But you look gorgeous.

24

I walk into Malik's office, don't even take the time to sit down, look him right in the eye and pull my hair back before I speak.

"I want to start my own leggings collection. And then produce a web series where I explain my creative process."

He looks at me, surprised. I thought of this on the way to his office. I am in no mood to beat around the bush today.

Grinning, he leans back in his chair.

"Your creative process?" he asks.

"Yes, they could follow me every step of the way from the initial idea to marketing. That way it wouldn't just be about leggings, it would be like ... the art of it. My art. Then I wouldn't just be a girl who sells stuff, and people would see that it goes deeper than that. Do you think we could get it on TV? If not, I could post it on my YouTube channel."

"Ellie, it may be rushing things to just —"

"I want to be prepared for the next step, Malik. So that in February, people see that I am in complete control of my own affairs. That I am doing great things. That just because Sam and I are finished doesn't mean I am, too. On the contrary. I am just getting started."

"Yes, but —"

"I'm ready. I will bounce back. We're going to bounce back. Besides, it was your idea! That I be my own brand! It can't be that complicated. You're the best, aren't you?"

"But the timing is not...I think that before undertaking anything, you need to step back a bit. There's no rush."

I don't know what comes over me. I lean my elbows on his desk, put my hands together in prayer, place my chin on the tips of my fingers and say what I've seen lots of actors do before me.

"The question is not whether I'm going to do this, Malik. The question is whether I am going to do it with or without you?"

Boom. I've stung him. He forces himself to smile.

It's a perfect little game, this duel between us. I work for him and he works for me.

He consults his computer screen.

"We would need to return to the basics. You haven't published many big things lately...I'm just telling you the way things are. You're on a downward trend right now, Ellie . . . and I'm worried."

I hold up my hand in front of me.

"I'll stop you there. I know that the last weeks have been difficult, but I'm better now. Doing really well! Sam and I have made a schedule for the apartment. I'm going there tomorrow and I'm preparing lots of content. I want to try out a new format, prepare recipes on Instagram Live. Everything is going to be fine from now on."

He takes a long sip of coffee and looks at me. Squints, studies me, as if he suspects I'm hiding something from him. I try to look good, fit, well rested, serene, even if am anything but. I smile but my mouth is dry. My head feels light and dense, like dryer lint.

I'm starting to run out of steam. I make an effort to get it back.

"I'm handling things. I will achieve my goals for the year. You'll see. I have plans for some incredible content in December."

I don't actually have a plan yet, but I'm talking without thinking because I don't want him to start listing all the things that I could be doing better, all the additional things I should be doing.

"A plan," he continues. "I know our goals were ambitious, but when I look at all the progress we've made this past year, I am very proud of you, Ellie. There's no point beating yourself over the head if —"

"No. I'm going to do it, I guarantee it. I've got a month to go. To make it to the top three."

Fake it till you make it, as they say. It will work out if I believe in it enough. It will happen.

Malik crosses his arms, skeptical. It's the first time that I've noticed his cologne, that he wears a bit too much of it. It smells like cheap vanilla. The odor makes me nauseous.

"Élisabeth, you're not going to buy Likes, are you?"

"Of course not! Honestly! Look. No. By the way, I'm spending two weeks in New Zealand with Mila from December 27. That should give me a little boost. I'm going to shoot lots of material."

"Yes, I know, that's great. I'm very happy that she asked you to collaborate with her on this trip."

Malik winks at me. He's proud of himself.

"You're welcome!" he adds.

It had occurred to me that it may not just have been Mila's idea to invite me.

"It's also not in small part due to me that it worked

out in the end," I say. "I was able to find more money. We're going to keep a journal for *Femme* magazine. Produce some exclusive content for their YouTube channel. That allowed us to negotiate a better package with the client. They should be sending the contracts for signature soon."

It's my turn to wink at him. "You're welcome!"

It was easy. They were thrilled at *Femme* and Banana Apparel. I didn't have to convince them... even though they wanted to pay for a plane ticket for Sam, too, but I declined, invented a recording session that would be difficult to get out of.

Malik is looking at me a bit too long for it to be natural.

"Are you okay, Ellie?" he asks, worried. "You're sleeping well? Eating well? Are you ready for your launch? Oh, and by the way, I have some excellent news."

"You have the presales numbers?"

"Better. Your publisher wants to release the second volume before the summer. And they've come up with a title. What do you think about..."

My throat tightens. Writing my book wasn't easy. I worked my ass off and didn't give myself a break.

I was so afraid that I was deceiving everyone, I lost sleep...

I'm not thrilled at the idea of doing it all again. Not so soon, in any case.

Malik takes a breath and sweeps his hand in the air front of him like a magician.

"*Sublime*," he whispers.

"For the title? Not bad, I'll think about it while I'm writing. But this summer is very soon."

"Exactly, but this time your editor will take care of everything. If you agree, they can start putting together the text quite quickly."

"What? I'm not going to write it?"

"Not exactly. Listen, Ellie, it took, what, a year for you to write *Radiant*? And then there was the job of revision... We can't wait so long this time. We have to feed your fans while they are still hungry. Who knows where things will be next year?"

"But...who's going to write it?"

"Don't worry. They've found a pro. Catherine-Audrey Rioux. They've already come up with a sample chapter for you to see! Of course, you'll brief her, make an outline. You're the one who has the final say, and they won't publish anything you haven't approved."

"Won't it be strange having her name on the book?"

Malik laughs. "It will be your name, my sweet. You are the one who is sublime."

"But isn't that, like, cheating?"

"Not at all! It's common practice, an old tradition. It's called using a ghost writer. Quite poetic, when you think about it."

I sigh. They've hired someone else to write my book. That means they were disappointed. If I had been good enough, they would want me to write the second book, of course.

I'm disappointed in myself. Very disappointed. I should have done better. But still...It's weird that it won't be me. Quinoa Forever is my story, my baby...

At the same time, I'd be relieved not to have this project on my plate along with everything else.

"Okay...But I can help her! I have recipes and lots of ideas for topics of —"

"Great, I'll tell them! Listen, they've sent me a proposed introduction and they want to know what you think. So make yourself a nice cup of herbal tea, put on your slippers and read this with a clear head. And then you can talk to me about it."

"Wow. Already, huh…"

"And the good news is that it will give you time to concentrate on other things like your leggings collection. I'll make some calls this afternoon and get back to you!"

I stand up, puzzled. I remain standing there in the middle of his office. Staring at nothing.

"Ellie, everything okay?" Malik says after several seconds.

I don't reply. I am hypnotized by the patterns on the carpet.

Time passes.

"My father is dying." I say it to hear myself say it. To imagine the world without him.

"Oh! I am sorry, Ellie, that's… I'm sorry."

"Thank you. It'll be okay. Everything is going to be fine."

SUBLIME
(Working title — *Radiant*, Volume 2)

By Catherine-Audrey Rioux for Élisabeth Bourdon-Marois

Wow, ~~lots of~~ so many things have happened since the publication of my first book! During it all, I discovered much more about myself and about different aspects of my life. I think that each day I am learning to know and accept myself ~~with all my faults~~ the way I am. But there is one thing that hasn't changed, and that is your support. So many of you have followed me on my platforms and supported me in my projects. I am truly grateful. Thank you for being there #TeamEllie ~~#gratitude~~.

For a long time I ~~hated my body~~ was at war with my body. I wanted to lose weight at any cost! I measured my success by the waist measurement of my jeans or the number of calories I consumed each day. Until the morning of my twenty-first birthday, after another desperate attempt to change my body by following yet another ridiculous diet (hello, cabbage soup, hello, not-so-intermittent fasting), when I decided that it was high time I began to ~~love myself and~~ take care of myself. To nourish myself on another level. I didn't know how I was going to do it, but the important thing was that that morning, I made a decision to ~~accept~~ love myself.

I had no idea I was about to embark on an adventure that

was going to bring me the physical and mental well-being that I ~~so desperately~~ needed, but also that my insights would turn into books! Today my job is to share the big and small moments of my life, my passions and my reflections and, in doing so, motivate ~~my followers~~ my community to adopt a healthy ~~active~~ lifestyle.

Those who know me know that I learn by trial and error (and I make lots of errors, believe me!). I always look for what works best for me and I'm happy to share the fruit of my experiences with you. But please, keep in mind that ~~everyone is different, and the world is perfect like that!~~ what works for me may not work for everyone.

My goal is to find the best food, the best fuel, to be the best version of myself, both physically and mentally! So if you're on board, let's get started! I will take you behind the scenes of my daily life, I'll share my recipes, my workouts and my favorite little routines that will make you feel good and rid yourself of that *&?%?! guilt.

Because being good to yourself is what being sublime is all about!

~~With all my love,~~ LOVE,

Elliexx

**Top 10 YouTubers
CAN/FR**

1. Jordanne Jacques – 808,000 followers
2. Tellement Cloé – 764,000 followers
3. Cath Bonenfant – 505,000 followers
4. Mila Mongeau – 504,000 followers
5. **Ellie – Quinoa Forever – 503,000 followers**
6. Emma & Juju – 498,000 followers
7. Approved by Gwen – 428,000 followers
8. Sophie Chen – 345,000 followers
9. Maëla Djeb – 166,000 followers
10. Zoé around the World – 148,000 followers

25

It was subtle at first, but now it's become very obvious. Opale is spying on me. I mean, this morning she got up at the same time as me. At seven o'clock.

Her nose in her phone, she drinks a giant cup of coffee as she keeps an eye on me. I eat breakfast while revising the checklist for my launch for the last time. It's tomorrow already, I haven't slept, it's stressing me out.

"It's funny," she says, "to see you here eating some weird oatmeal…"

"I replace the oats with red lentils."

"Ah, anyway, it's funny because according to my feed, you're busy preparing a smoothie made of acai berries in your perfect kitchen with your popular boyfriend."

Proud of her little dig, she gives me a toothy smile while showing me a photo that I just posted. She goes so far as to read the captions in a high-pitched squeaky voice.

"I just love taking my time in the morning to savor a breakfast brimming with @Karma superfoods like acai berries and ginger."

"I don't talk like that!"

I laugh. I've decided that I'm not going to let Opale's infinitely variable sense of humor ruin my life. I just take her the way she is. Like a grumpy old tomcat, but declawed.

"I didn't know I had the pleasure of counting you as one of my followers," I say.

"I use a pseudonym. I don't release my personal information to predatory multinationals."

I look at her, a little exasperated, take a big swallow of my hot lemon with a dash of cayenne pepper without blinking an eye. It stings the back of my throat but I tough it out and don't cough.

Opale returns to her cell, satisfied, and I tell myself that she and Alice make a good couple. I'm happy that they've got over their little fight from the other night.

With a smile, I whisper, "I heard that Mark Zuckerberg eats baby dolphins for lunch."

Without lifting her eyes from her screen, she replies, "I heard that acai berries are just big blueberries cultivated ten thousand kilometers from here by workers under precarious conditions, and overhyped by rich White guys to make women believe that by eating them they can lose weight or even look more youthful, but did you know that their effectiveness has never actually been tested?"

"Opale."

"Yes?"

"You are exhausting. Don't you want to take a little break from time to time, relax, live in the present moment?"

"Not at all. Is that what you do?"

"No."

I go back to my to-do list.

"But," she says, "explain to me why you continue to post stuff like that? You don't like your boyfriend, food stresses you out constantly, and you cry nonstop."

"Yes, but, no. It's temporary. I don't have the choice to... I don't have any choice. That's the way it is."

Unimpressed, she looks straight at me and says, "You know, Ellie, it's funny, but ever since you came here, there's been a scale in our bathroom."

She stares at me with big eyes, super serious. I don't know what to say. It's absurd.

"Well, yeah. I weigh myself. So?"

"You work out twice a day."

"My book launch is tomorrow. I want to be in good shape."

"There's nothing but green vegetables and nuts in your groceries."

"So okay, look! You may have never seen a vegetable here before, but it would do you good to try them."

"I think you have a problem."

"Agh, if I have a 'problem,' it would mean that there are quite a few of us here who have a problem…"

I'm laughing as I say this, making like it doesn't bother me. There is no way I'm going to justify myself. I don't have a "problem." I just do what I've always been taught to do, that's all. I watch my weight. Because for me, if I stop being obsessed with what I eat, that will always mean not being at my "ideal weight." If I ate when I was hungry, exercised in a reasonable way and just lived, I would put on weight. My body is set like that. I would get fat again. Not fat in my own head, but fat for real. And if the past twenty-five years have taught me anything, it's that being fat is the worst thing that I could do to humanity.

So I watch my weight, and I would like people to leave me alone about it. I don't want to deal with negative comments, uncomfortable looks, being criticized. I don't have the courage to face that right now. Today I just want to believe in my own bullshit, the idea that being thin will take care of the problem.

Opale takes a sip of coffee. The noise she makes when she drinks gets on my nerves.

"As for you, I think you have a problem with alcohol, but I'm not going to get on your case about it."

"Yes, you're right. Without a doubt. Also pot. And I watch way too much Netflix for my own good. All the same, I wouldn't trade places with you!"

"Ha, ha. Me neither!...Me neither." Still, I feel the need to justify myself. "It's because I signed up for a challenge, that's all."

"It's an intensive weight-loss program, not a 'challenge.'"

I knew it. She's spying on me. I knew it!

"Okay, maybe. But I am not normally that extreme. I...it's temporary. I'm just doing what I have to do."

"For?"

"For...because that's what people expect of me!

I don't have any choice but to do it … You can't understand."

"But no one cares! You are not obliged to do a thing. The world really doesn't need another privileged influencer telling them what to eat or how to fit the mold! You're just doing what you do for yourself. At least admit that much!"

I bury my head in my hands. I don't know what to think anymore. Whatever I do is wrong.

"Ugh. I just want to have a quiet breakfast," I say, rubbing my eyes. "If you don't mind. Just live my life. I didn't ask for any of this this morning."

"Okay, okay."

She shrugs her shoulders, raises her hands, nods her head in a sign of truce, goes back to her phone.

"You know," she says, "I understand that you are not a bad person deep down."

"…"

"You're a victim of a capitalist society and the diet culture, and it's true that you can't place the blame for an odious systemic problem on the shoulders of a single influencer, even if practically speaking, what you do is super problematic and has consequences…"

I rub my face vigorously with the palms of my hands and pray that Alice will get up before noon.

"Opale, a bit of peace and quiet, I beg you! Please."

"Yeah, yeah, sorry, I'll stop, but just to say I think you should put blueberries in your recipes. It's exactly the same thing as acai but it's local and you wouldn't be encouraging the use of —"

"Okay, I'm going to go and take a shower."

"Four minutes of hot water, don't forget."

"I won't."

"The planet will thank you!"

"The planet is my friend! Yay!"

PAPA

I am thirteen years old. It's summer and I'm wasting my vacation at the cottage, away from my friends. Alice has become BFFs with the neighbor. They're the same age, they play together.

I, on the other hand, am bored. I spend my time on the swing at the end of the balcony. My old kiddie swing. I put on my headphones, hang on to the ropes, push myself forward. I close my eyes. My body swings, and I'm flying, dreaming, inventing a life for myself.

I have a favorite scenario, where I am a champion figure skater competing in the nationals. I hear my name echo through the rink. It's my turn, my big moment. I jump on the ice, throw my arms in the air and wave to the crowd. I'm wearing a sparkly costume, lipstick, my hair is tied back in a French braid.

I'm skating to Vivaldi. "Summer" or "Winter" — doesn't matter. Starting position, double bass. One, two, three, four. My skates caress the ice, I glide, I float expertly. My arms twirl in the air.

Harpsichord. One, two, three, four. Pirouette with an arched back. Stag jump. Double axel.

Violins. One, two, three, four. Split jump. Double toe loop. Triple lutz.

Violas. One, two, three, four. Camel spin. Sit spin. Not even out of breath yet.

One, two, three, four. I skate like a feather, like the wind.

One, two, three, four. A spectacular combination. One, two, three, four.

And then it's the grand finale. One, two, three, four. I attempt a triple axel. I lean in. The crowd holds their breath. So does the television commentator. One, two, three, four. I twist in the air. Once, twice, three times. I land in an arabesque. Yes! I glide into my final position. Powerful, moving. I did it. I melt in a deep curtsy, the crowd goes wild. My parents are proud. Flowers rain down, stuffed animals. I wave to my fans in gratitude. The judges are about to give their —

On the other end of the porch, my father waves and signals to me to take off my headphones.

I obey.

"Come for a bike ride," he says.

I give him an annoyed look as usual.

"Oh, Papa! Noooo! I don't want to."

"Come on."

"Okay."

I stop the swing, put on my shoes, drag my feet to my bike stored under the balcony. It's full of mud and long-legged spiders. My father watches me with an amused look. I put on my helmet and get on my bike. He does the same.

We ride — him in the front, me behind. Together. Our faces whipped by the wind, our shoulders splashed with sunshine. I don't hate it. He speeds up, and I have to pedal faster to keep up with him, one, two, three, four. It's hard. I'm out of breath. One, two, three, four. I'm hot. One, two, three, four. I'm thirsty, need a break.

We stop beside Pierre and Anne's house, our friends. Pierre is busy painting his porch. My father puts a foot on the ground, waves. I force myself to smile, to look friendly. My parents think I don't smile enough lately.

After a drink of water, my father says, "Pierre, you're at it again."

"Hi there, Jacques! What a beautiful day, I'm taking advantage of it! What brings you this way?"

"I'm taking my daughter out for a ride. She needs it."

I lower my eyes, stare at the little stones on the ground.

She needs it.

The sun presses me onto my seat. I sink heavily into the gravel. My eyes slide down to my thighs, my belly.

No, I don't dare look at myself. My father's scolding voice in my head as I take in the tall grass, the river at low tide. I feel the tide rising inside me. I want to dive in and lose myself in it. To forget.

That he's taking me for a ride. That I have to lose weight.

One, two, three, four.

I have to lose weight.

#MOTIVATION

Your body is a masterpiece in the making.

You have everything you need, but it's going to take everything you have.

You're not going to get the butt of your dreams by sitting on it.

NO EXCUSES.

It doesn't get any easier, you just get stronger.

You may hurt tomorrow or you may be unhappy tomorrow, it's your choice.

We only get what we deserve with hard work and perseverance.

Do it again and again until it's part of you.

Become the person no one thought you could be.

Ideal weight: Sexy as f*ck.

If you're tired, do it tired.

When you eat crap, you feel like crap.

Keep going. You didn't make it this far just to make it this far.

It's easier to wake up in the morning and work out than look in the mirror every day and not love what you see.

YOU GO, GIRL.

You're not tired, you're inspired.

26

"Ellie, your speech was so moving!"

Mila puts her hand on her heart, talks to me like we are the only two people in the room. She's into the moment, but I am overwhelmed. My eyes scan the crowd that has gathered for my book launch. Conversations ring in my ears. Around us, servers circulate with trays filled with cups of chai tea, turmeric smoothies and chocolate chip cookies made with chickpea flour — my signature recipe.

The Karma team has been kind enough to host us in their new office. It is an incredible airy, open space with huge windows, concrete columns and a breathtaking view of downtown. They agreed to take care of all the logistics. Which is fortunate because I no longer know which way is up. We've invited a lot of people. The place is full of influencers, celebrities big and small, winners of my contests, columnists, buyers, sponsors, my family, the whole team from my agency and even a few booktubers chosen by the PR person.

The idea is that the book should be EVERYWHERE on the networks tonight.

I try to spot familiar faces among the crowds of

people in the open room, but Mila is talking very fast, and I'm having a hard time concentrating.

"When you were reading the passage from your book about how life is too short not to become the best version of yourself, that you have to know your roots if you are going to blossom, that was so inspiring for me!"

"Yeah...it's crazy. I feel like I wrote that a million years ago."

"You must be so proud!"

"Well, not really. I could have done better, I think."

"I'm freaking out that New Zealand is coming up so soon. Have you had any news?"

I'm already exhausted, and the evening is far from over. I have to talk louder than usual to make myself heard.

"Oh, yes, don't worry. Souad from Banana Apparel promised me that the contracts would be sent for signature at the beginning of the week, latest."

I scan the room, looking for a way to extract myself from Mila. Nothing against her, she's super great, but I think I just saw Simon Ouellet with his girlfriend, La Petite Sophie, in line for the make-your-own energizing granola bar, and I'd really like to say hello.

We wanted to have something "wow" for the event. I liked the idea on paper, but it's not quite as wow as I thought. I was thinking more like, you know, a pyramid of champagne glasses? Charlotte Cardin? Virtual reality?

No. An energizing granola bar. And I have no swag.

Mila is practically vibrating with joy.

"Oh, my God, I'm so excited! Thanks for following up. I've just been so slammed with things lately!"

"It's nothing."

"Secret project. I can't talk about it."

"Cool."

I'm surprised to see the twins Emma and Juju in the corner where there are hammocks and rocking chairs, in deep conversation with Sarah Coutu. Sarah has just had her vegan coming-out, so I had no choice but to invite her.

"Okay, fine," Mila whispers in my ear. "I'll tell you, but it stays between us! I'm going to publish a book, too. It's going to be about the hidden side of social media!" She pretends to zip up her lips.

"Ah. That's...original. Congrats!"

In the distance, I see my mother arriving on the

arm of Nico. Her complexion is the color of . . . a clementine. Is it the Mexican sun or tanning lotion? Doesn't matter, I'm happy to see her. I was getting bored.

Alice is already making her way toward her, relieved to finally see someone she can talk to.

It's my cue.

"My mother has just arrived," I say to Mila. "Can we pick this up later?"

"Of course, go on, this is your big night, my friend!"

Did she just say "my friend"? It warms my heart.

I give her a wink.

"See you soon, my friend."

I'd decided to ghost my nutrition coach, Josiane, after our last meeting. She was just too . . . intense.

But I forgot to take her off the invitation list for this evening. I am such a crap ghost.

When I saw her arrive, I did my best to avoid her, dodge her smiles, her looks, her little waves. But now she's heading straight for me with her personalized bag of granola.

She decides to open the conversation with a tasty observation.

"They're already out of pumpkin seeds, can you believe it?"

I think I can. I smile at her, and she gives me big cheek kisses.

"Well, well, well!" she says. "I see someone who has taken her health into her own hands, it seems. I'm proud of you. You must come by the office. I always say, it's not how many times you fall down, but how many times you get up again."

I find this idea that you must never quit kind of irritating — when it comes from someone other than me.

"As I always say," she goes on enthusiastically, "the distance between reality and your dreams is called…?"

"Uh…I don't know."

"Just guess, for fun."

"Despair?"

"Of course not! Action!"

I imagine how satisfying it would feel to start pelting her with little raisins. To flick them in her face, one raisin at a time.

"I was worried," she whispers, widening her eyes,

"that you were moving dangerously away from your healthy weight, but look at you! You're back on track! Don't even have to weigh yourself to know that you don't have much more to lose."

"I have to go . . ." I say politely. "I . . . have this thing to . . . see you soon!"

I give her a thumbs-up as I get away as quickly as possible.

It's funny. I don't know which of us needs help more.

I hang around the energizing granola bar looking for someone to talk to. A girl wearing an emerald green velvet top and red lips walks toward me with a lot of determination.

I wave at her from a distance. While I watch her approach, Josiane's words echo in my head: *You don't have much more to lose . . .*

How much more?

I breathe out, look around. I can't seem to relax, enjoy myself. Since the beginning of the evening, I feel like I'm missing out on the good conversations, never being in the right place, never with the right people. I'm looking for fun, trying to feel like I'm at my own book launch, but I don't find it anywhere.

The girl in the green crop top is standing in front of me, and I realize that she has probably been talking to me for several seconds, and I have no idea what about.

"Excuse me, remind me what your name is?"

"Odile!"

"Nice to meet you, Odile."

"But we already know each other. I'm a blogger!"

"Right, excuse me, there are so many people here. I'm sorry, I lost my train of thought. Of course I remember…"

I have no idea. I am saved by one of the servers who offers us a bite to eat. Odile jumps at the chance, rushes to the tray and takes as many cups and little plates as possible.

It makes me smile, and I remember my first events as a blogger, how I also used to love getting free stuff. I was flattered by all the invitations, thought I was part of the in crowd.

Now I understand that it was just based on the number of my followers. I don't know Odile, but I invited her to my launch. I invited her for the number of her followers.

I'm buying influence, too.

Odile takes a bite of cookie, chews for a long time and makes a funny face when she swallows. Very politely, she places her little paper cup on one of the bistro tables and takes a big gulp of chai. She smiles, embarrassed.

I freeze. The air in my lungs is like liquid, viscous.

I excuse myself, promise to return, chase after the server thinking, Holy crap, the Karma team ruined my recipe.

I grab a cookie, taste it, taste again. Shit, no!

It's not good, not good at all. I look for Joëlle, the Karma coordinator, in the crowd. Try to look relaxed, smile at the people who turn to me as I pass.

I find her in the LAB, a kind of glassed-in kitchen space where the team develops new products.

"Did you change the cookie recipe?" I ask, my voice shaky.

"No, we followed it to the letter..."

"That's impossible, they are not good. They don't taste the way they usually do."

"But...I think they taste delicious...the way they usually do."

I don't even bother to reply. I leave, accost a server, take two more cookies and go looking for Sam. I have to make my way by gently dodging everyone who wants to congratulate me. It's like trying to walk in water one difficult step at a time.

I finally find him in a deep conversation with Mila, leaning against a concrete post.

I don't even wait until they finish. I just hand him a cookie.

"Taste this."

"Okay, what?"

"It tastes different, doesn't it?"

Always the charmer, he shakes back his hair, smiles at Mila. I watch him take a bite with his eyes closed, as if he's taking his task really seriously.

"Tastes like usual," he says.

"Impossible. The texture, there's a taste…it tastes like chickpeas."

"Well…it's made with chickpeas."

He looks at Mila as if for confirmation, to make her smile.

It works. She laughs, crosses her arms, frowns, watches me. It annoys me, but this is not the moment to lose it. This is my big evening, all eyes on me, and I need to stay calm.

Breathe through the nose, Ellie, breathe.

"Yes, except it doesn't taste . . . you're not supposed to taste it. That's the concept . . . Never mind. It's all good. Everything's cool. I'll . . . I'll be back."

My heart is beating quickly. I can barely catch my breath, my throat is closing up. I've had too much tea.

The bathroom, I need to find the bathroom. To calm down.

Otherwise the whole world will see. The whole world will understand that things are not okay. Not at all.

"My sweetie, I've been looking for you everywhere. I want to introduce you to Lison! She was my good friend in high school, can you believe that she works for your publisher?"

My mother freezes when she sees me crouching behind the boxes of books in the small meeting room where I put my things when I arrived.

I'm hiding out here. The plan was to calm myself down, but that isn't working at all. I'm hot, my left arm feels numb, my heart is pounding so hard that I feel sick.

"Maman," I say. "How do you know if you're having a heart attack?"

Just hearing myself say heart attack makes me panic.

"Who…what?"

"I hurt here." I point to my chest.

She looks at me, confused. I've caught her off guard.

She puts her hand on my head, pats it with her fingers.

"This is a lot of stress for you, all this. It's…a big night."

She's uncomfortable. It's too much for her, dealing with my emotions. I try to catch my breath and explain.

"The cookie recipe has never been good! And Sam, we're not…anymore, we…"

"Wait here, don't move. I'm going to find him!"

"No!"

I want to tell her not to do it, to at least go and find Alice, but she's already gone. She's taken off like a deer from a hunter, saving her own skin.

But what about me? Am I dying?

235

Sam arrives quickly, puts his smoothie on the meeting-room table, kneels down and holds my head, looks me in the eyes.

"I can't...catch...my breath."

Mila has come in, too, and she stands behind him.

"Ellie, you're having a panic attack," she says reassuringly. "Breathe, I promise that it will stop, it's just a bad moment. Breathe. I get them, too, and they always pass."

"I'm...not...going to die?"

Sam takes me in his arms, laughs softly.

"You are not going to die. I'm here," he says.

I lean into him, hug him tightly. His smell, his warmth, the softness of his sweater, it calms me. I manage to inhale, exhale, inhale again. And it gets easier and easier. My heart rate slows down.

Mila says she's going to leave us, that she'll be right next door if I need her. It's like she's waiting for me to ask her to stay, but no. I want to be alone with Sam.

He rocks me for a long time, and it helps to calm me down.

After a few minutes, he presses his forehead against mine, wipes away my tears.

"Is this because of the cookies?" he asks.

"No. Yes. I don't know. It's everything. Everything has been so fucked up this past month."

"Yeah, tell me about it."

We just stay there in silence, and then I say, "We should get out of here before someone finds us. I don't want to go back out there. I don't feel well."

"But it's your party, Ellie. You've worked so hard to be here…"

His smile is infinitely soft.

I wipe my nose on my sleeve, hiccuping.

"They've started to write the second volume of my book without me. The girl who's writing it says stuff and it's like I'm the one who's talking, but it's not me."

"Wait…that's absurd. We can stop that. Malik will take care of it!"

"No, no need…I wish I could tell you that it doesn't make sense, that it's bad, but it's exactly the stuff I would write…it's fluff. What I do is fluff."

"What? No!"

"Yes. I chew over the same clichés that everyone has heard a thousand times about wellness and self-care. I want to believe it so much, but the worst part is that it's not even true! It's not true that I've found myself or that I'm doing well, you know what I mean?"

Just saying it feels freeing. I become lighter, I breathe.

"For days I haven't been eating when I'm hungry, Sam. I wake up at night feeling hungry. And that makes me happy, I'm proud of myself! How twisted is that?"

He looks up at the ceiling, worried, holds me in his arms, then looks into my eyes.

"I'm sorry."

"For what?"

"I was a real asshole. I am a real asshole. You can look any way you want, Ellie. The problem is not you, it's me."

I flinch. This is a lot, coming out of nowhere.

"What do you mean?"

"I'm not saying this to try to get you to change your mind about the two of us, okay? I respect your decision. But I've come to understand a lot of things since you left. Everything is so flat without you. I miss our projects, our team."

I sniffle, straighten up.

"Understand things like what, for instance?"

"Well...lots of things..."

"Like what, exactly?"

He hesitates, and I get the feeling he's not super comfortable talking about this, especially here.

He looks around, gathers his courage.

"Okay. Well…I…I realize that I have always been around beautiful girls…girls who everyone thinks are beautiful. That was a given. I always loved what that said about me, to be that guy."

"Okay."

"But with you, Ellie…it's not the same. You're not like those other girls for me. I've never been in a relationship for that long…Just that, it's not nothing!"

"No, of course…"

"You are super, super beautiful! But…when I think of you putting on weight, I don't know whether you're beautiful anymore. Wait, I'm not saying that you aren't! I'm saying that I lose my bearings. Then, yes, I got scared. I got scared about what that said about me."

"Oh. Great."

"No, but I'm the one who's not cool. Who needs to prove myself through you. As if that makes me something less if you aren't 'perfect.' How can I be such an asshole?"

"Enough already. We make a good pair of assholes."

He laughs.

"Except, I realize that I love you no matter what. I'm not asking you for anything, I just want you to know that. I love you no matter what."

"Okay," I say, a bit stunned.

"Okay," Sam says.

"Okay, okay." It's the only thing that comes out of my mouth.

We sit there in silence.

"Stay…" he says. "You deserve to have the most beautiful launch, for this to be the best night of your life. You can't leave now."

I laugh, while rubbing my fingers under my eyes to check for running mascara. Sam smiles at me ruefully.

He's here. I feel that he's here beneath all the layers. I see it, he's sincere.

We look at each other, and it makes me feel good to find him. He calms me.

I realize he's looking at my lips, and he leans in to kiss me. I turn my head and his mouth lands on my cheek.

"Uh, I'm not there in my head yet. I…sorry."

He pouts, rubs his hand over his face. I feel bad. He smiles, swallows his disappointment, holds out his smoothie.

"I understand. Are you hungry? Do you want some of my delicious turmeric smoothie?"

"But does it taste like turmeric?"

"Well," he says uneasily. "Yeah. It is turmeric."

"That was a joke, Sam."

He smiles. "Oh, okay! It's funny. You're funny."

I laugh, realize it's a side of my personality that I don't often show him. I take a little sip. He holds out his hand and smiles.

"Come on, I promise you, it will be okay. We'll have fun."

He's right. We have a nice evening.

When I'm with him, everything is easy.

∞

At the end, while the Karma team takes care of all the cleaning up, I pass by the granola bar. I'm the last one. There are just a few pieces of maple tempeh and a bowl full of prunes.

Sam comes over with our coats, leans over and whispers in my ear.

"I know a place. It's quite a nicely decorated apartment…the guy who lives there plays the guitar and gives excellent foot massages. I think you'd find him cute even though he does often leave his socks lying around."

He passes his hand through his hair. He is beautiful — the most beautiful, no question.

I bite my lip, finish wiping the granola counter with a big cloth that smells like citrus. I try to think, but I'm tired. My brain feels like an orange passing through the juicer.

"Interesting offer…but for tonight, I'd rather you drop me at the metro."

David Lanctôt has sent you a message

D: Have I already told you about my recipe for shepherd's pie with cheese curds and ketchup chips?

E: You know that I could report you to the public health authorities for that.

D: I'm shaking.

E: Mr. Lanctôt, you are under arrest. This recipe contravenes the recommendations of Canada's Food Guide.

D: I plead not guilty, Your Honor. There are tomatoes in ketchup. See for yourself!

E: Hahaha. Idiot.

PAPA

It's my birthday. I am ten years old. My mother has made me a dress. A big girl's dress, a woman's dress. Pale blue. A row of buttons down the front — buttons in the form of small white flowers.

It's magnificent. My mother was up all night making the final adjustments. She's worked hard to finish her birthday gift to me.

I put it on and parade around the living room. Proud. Today is my day. Today I am special. I am beautiful, too. I'm wearing a dress that was made for me, just for me. It's one of a kind. Just look.

My father doesn't like the dress. He tells my mother this. It's not to hurt my feelings, it's just that he doesn't like it. It doesn't suit me. He can't pretend otherwise. The dress isn't flattering. Not for my "body type." He's saying this for my own good.

My mother suggests something else. A dress that I've already worn twenty thousand times. Bought in a store. A dress just like thousands of others. It's ridiculous for someone's tenth birthday. It has big yellow sunflowers. Ridiculous.

Everything is ruined. I wear my new dress anyway,

but I don't think I look good in it now. It's impossible to see it through the same eyes as before.

Today I will not be special. Today I will be the same as yesterday. The same as tomorrow.

I wear my body, Papa, like a dress you don't like.

27

I arrive on time with a zucchini loaf. Ready to lose at Scrabble, ready to tell my father that I love him. I've waited too long already.

I take off my boots, take in his news. The doctor has adjusted his medication. The following week, he will go to the cottage. He's made his decision. He wants to die at the cabin. He has hired a nurse, a caregiver. It's difficult for him to be on his own. His condition is deteriorating, it's impossible to take a shower, but going to the hospital is out of the question. The worst thing is the nausea. The worst thing is the dry mouth.

I soak up the silence, resist the urge to run away.

"I love you, Papa," I say.

Slowly, he gets up from his armchair, opens his arms in gratitude. I breathe in his smell of sweat and cologne. I snuggle against him. I want it to be a good moment. His mouth in my hair, he speaks like each word is going to be his last.

"You are a woman now, my coco-pomme. I am proud of you."

He covers my head with urgent little kisses, holds

me tightly in his arms. I give in, and feel like a spectator to our final moments. A zucchini loaf, a game of Scrabble, "I love you," and we say no more. It's too late, in any case. Too late for me to feel anything more than reconciled, relieved.

I look out the window, see the snow falling in timid little flakes. It melts, forgotten as soon as it hits the ground.

I pull myself away from his arms, help him sit down, put a cushion behind his back.

"I didn't know you were proud of me," I say, trying to make light of my emotions. "Honestly, I didn't know it was even possible!"

I burst out laughing, and I start to cry.

No. I wipe my eyes, force myself to smile, take the Scrabble box and place it in front of him. He's confused. I continue as we planned with our social game and healthy snack, with the idea of having a moment of father-daughter bonding. As if we've done it before, as if it was still possible.

He looks at me silently, astonished. Part of me tells myself to keep my mouth shut. The other part of me doesn't care.

"It's just that...I know that you're sick, but I find

it difficult to pretend that things have been different between us. As if you had ever been proud of me or —"

He cuts me off.

"Look, coco-pomme —"

"Stop with that… stop it. You haven't called me that in a fucking long time."

I occupy my hands setting up the game board, getting out two little racks from the box. I sit down. My hands are shaking. I draw seven tiles from the pink cotton bag and pass it to my father.

I'm searching for words.

"It's just made me realize that… all this time, you were able to do it but you didn't. Not once, Papa… did I feel… that you loved me."

He stays silent, his body weak, his gaze hard. I'm afraid I've made him angry. I line up my letters on the rack in front of me. I try to put them in order. I move them around, as if by mixing them up enough, I could make them form a word that makes sense.

"It is because I love you," he says. "I was hard with you… because I love you, to show you that you were capable of big things, Élisabeth, that I believed in you."

I put my hand in front of my mouth. I've already said too much. My father fidgets on his chair. He's sad, his words are shaky, he's out of breath.

"Look at the woman you have become today...You succeed in absolutely everything you undertake..."

I want to interrupt, but he gestures for me to let him finish.

"Would you have preferred...that I let you settle for less?"

It hurts me, the idea that I would be less without him. I get up awkwardly, knocking my chair to the ground. I give it a big kick.

My anger surprises me. I feel like screaming, but I put my hand in front of my mouth to stifle my words.

"Fuck off!"

My father closes his eyes. He's exasperated.

"Very well, Élisabeth. You can leave."

I wipe my tears, pick up the chair, stand it upright. Hesitate. Start to pack up the game, put the letters in the bag, the racks in the box.

I stop and take a deep breath.

"I'm going to make you dinner first. Help you take a shower if you want. Then I'll come over as often as you need me. Except if we are going to do this, if we're going to try to say goodbye properly, then I want to be able to be honest. That's all I ask. That I have the right to my truth."

"Very well," he says, his voice tight. "Enlighten us with your truth."

It's now or never.

"I am fragile, not strong."

I feel him soften. I try to collect my thoughts, to express them adequately. I'm afraid that my words will fail to convey what I feel.

"I feel like I was never good enough for you," I continue. "Never up to that level, but I have tried again and again — so much that I don't know who I am anymore outside the idea of succeeding or pleasing or performing. I don't know how to exist any other way, but I never got the feeling that I was good enough. No matter what I do, I feel like a failure. I think that things will fill me up but no, compliments aren't enough, being successful is never big enough, nothing lasts, nothing feels good."

His eyes are fixed on me. I don't know what he's thinking, but at least he's listening to me. I am overcome with a huge feeling of fatigue.

"I did my best," he says.

I go over, kneel down, put my hand on his.

"I don't doubt it. Not for a second, Papa." I hold his gaze. "But I get the feeling that you've never needed the approval of others, not the way I need it. You've always done things your way, always been strong. I would have loved to learn from you how to be like that. To be free like you."

I'm crying, and for the first time in a long time, they are healing tears.

"Even though I'm angry, I'm going to miss you like crazy, Papa. I don't want you to go."

86 NEW MESSAGE REQUESTS

tania.soleil

OMG. I really think you should look at these photos . . .

maude_julie

I'm so sorry, but I think you need to know . . .

sylvainflamand2016

Nasty piece of trash, your boyfriend . . .

sarahmichelle

Hi Ellie, are they kissing???

soraya_d

IS THAT SAM?!!!!

juliet.romeo

Maybe it's none of my business, but are you still going out with . . .

see more

28

"It's Britney, bitch."

I do Becky Robins' "20-minute Killer Booty Burn." My thighs are on fire, I go lower and lower in a perfect squat. I hold the position. I engage my glutes, propel myself with the help of my legs. Jump squat. I absorb the impact and start again. Squat, jump, squat, jump.

In my headphones, I hear Becky Robins say that it's time to "take it up to tempo." I pick up the pace. My heart pounds to the beat of the music. *"Gimme gimme more, gimme more…"* I imitate each of Becky's moves on the screen. She smiles, I smile. She adjusts her ponytail, I adjust my ponytail. I move in perfect synchronicity. I forget myself in her, I become Becky Robins. Jump lunges one, two, three, four. I take off, I fly, close my eyes, empty my thoughts, at last. Emptiness.

I forget that Sam and Mila were seen together in a bar, kissing. *"Gimme more, gimme more…"*

"They want more? Well, I'll give them more." Jump lunges, one, two, three, four.

I feel someone's presence, open my eyes, stop cold.

Opale is standing there looking at me, completely bowled over by the spectacle unfolding in front of her eyes. The spectacle that is me.

I take off my headphones. I'm a little embarrassed. Opale smiles, rubs her eyes.

"What in the world are you doing?" she asks. "It's not even 5:00 a.m."

I drop down to my mat on all fours, like a little animal.

"I'm trying to become a morning person," I say, trying to catch my breath.

"Are you kidding me?"

"Yes. I just wanted to see your reaction."

"It worked."

"I'm starting to get to know you. Did I wake you?"

"No. Alice snores."

"Agh, I know! It's hell. She snores like a tractor, and if you have the misfortune to open your eyes in the middle of the night, it's all over, impossible to get back to sleep."

"So, like, what's going on?" Opale says softly.

I watch Becky Robins shake it up on my computer screen. She's doing donkey kicks like a machine. I don't hear anything, but I can read her lips, imagine her in the middle of saying, "Don't quit on yourself, Ellie! Look at my ass! You want a booty like this or what?"

I roll my eyes, stop the video.

"I can't sleep. My ex who isn't my ex yet is sleeping with my supposed best friend. And the whole world knows about it."

She takes time to take in this information, puts it together that I'm talking about Sam and Mila.

"Ouch," she says.

"People are sending me the same two blurry photos taken of them kissing in a bar. I think I got them about a hundred times last night, and they keep coming. My followers want to warn me."

"Wow, that's…"

"…because what I do for a living is super problematic and blah, blah, blah. I know."

"No! I mean, that's shit."

"Oh. Yeah. Thanks."

"How are you feeling?"

I think about it. It's not so simple in my head.

"I feel betrayed…" I begin.

"No doubt."

"Angry."

"That's predictable."

"You're predictable!"

"Ha, ha. Bravo, you're starting to catch on."

"Thank you. And...jealous."

"That one's more surprising."

I wipe my face with my microfiber towel.

"When I was brushing my teeth earlier, I was so hungry, I went to take my gummy vitamin, and I ate the whole bottle. Whatever was left in it, anyway."

Her mouth twists into a little grimace. She feels sorry for me.

"Do you think it's dangerous to overdose on vitamin E?" I ask.

"That depends."

"Zinc?"

"Maybe. How many did you eat?"

"I don't know. Maybe ten."

"Okay, you'll live, but for God's sake, Ellie, eat something! I'm going to make you some breakfast."

"No, it's all good. I ate after that. For real. I had a bowl of cereal. The cereal with the sailor who says, 'It's cruncharific!' on the box. I'm not proud of that, either."

This almost makes her smile.

"Did you replace the milk with kombucha?"

"Not even."

"Okay. That's good to hear."

She turns to leave. I stop her.

"Do you want to watch Netflix with me? Your documentary about serial killers, I think it would help me sleep."

"Good idea. I'm up to the episode about the Wyoming slasher, but first I have to go pee. Then I'm confiscating your other vitamin bottles. You can buy gummies at the convenience store like everyone else."

I watch her shuffle to the bathroom.

It's official. I like her.

CELEBRITY WORLD

[RUMOR] Is it all over between Sam and Ellie of Quinoa Forever?

Oh, no! Rumors have been rife on the web ever since the handsome singer from the band Monday was seen kissing influencer Mila Mongeau in a downtown bar. The couple, who got engaged earlier this month, still hadn't announced a date for their wedding. A coincidence? We hope that . . .

Samantha Larochelle introduces us to her lover and we're smitten!

We are in love with Samantha Larochelle, and we're obviously not the only ones! In fact, the singer-actress, author, influencer, woman of many talents, recently found love in the arms of a beautiful redhead. This weekend we were finally treated to the adorable smile of Samantha's mysterious lover. Impossible not to fall in love with her ourselves . . .

Selena St-Aubin pays tribute to . . . her dog!

#MlleGaufrette, Selena St-Aubin's little pooch, is getting on. The furry beauty recently celebrated her 15th birthday, and although the influencer and entertainer doesn't want to believe her adventures with her pup are over, she also knows all too well that time is running out. In a touching Instagram post dedicated to her dog, Selena recalls . . .

You have sent a message to Samuel Vanasse

E: How did you put it last time? Oh yes. I can't believe your lack of judgment on this matter.

E: Oh and also, your big beautiful speech about love the other night . . . big fat BULLSHIT, right?

S: I will explain it to you.

S: Stop fooling around. Please reply!

David Lanctôt sent you a message

D: Come over for dinner, Quinoa. I finish early tonight.

E: Tonight. Are you serious?

D: Very. Lasagna?

E: You don't have . . . a new girlfriend or whatever?

D: It's over with Florence.

E: Ah . . . sorry to hear that. Are things okay or are you having a hard time?

D: It's fine. It's never easy, but I think it's for the best ;)

E: Yes. I know what you mean . . . It's finished with Sam ;)

E: Well, I had been planning on arranging my spices in alphabetical order this evening, but, sure, I'm super game for dinner!

29

I've looked at the pictures of Sam and Mila 350,000 times. They are blurry. There are two theories circulating. The first, most obvious: they're kissing, no doubt about it. The second, oddly popular with my followers, is that we're wrong. They're just talking, and because the music is really, really loud, they have to talk really, really close to each other's mouths... with her touching his chest, him holding her neck.

In short, I don't doubt for a second that they are kissing in the photos. But even if they're just talking, I imagine that they made plans to meet in the bar after my launch, and it was not to play Skip-Bo.

I was right! I was right to think Sam wasn't being honest. To doubt him, his marriage proposal, his feelings.

It's just... I don't know that it makes me feel good knowing that. I mean, yes, I left him. I'd even been leading a double life for a while... But do I have the right to be angry? Jealous? I don't know. It's too much to handle at the moment.

So I ignore his calls. I wouldn't know what to say to him, except maybe swear a bit.

As for Mila, it changes from minute to minute. Sometimes I hate her. Sometimes I feel sorry for her. For how much attention she needs. I almost texted her but I changed my mind. Thank heavens we haven't yet signed the contracts for New Zealand. Thank you, God.

Of course, Malik called me. He asked me to hold off before reacting publicly. It would seem the best strategy in this kind of situation is to do nothing. That the less you comment on the rumor, the less traction it will get on gossip sites and the fewer opportunities there will be for people to talk about it. In short, he promised to manage the main stakeholders and to report back quickly.

As for me, I swore to keep quiet on my own networks.

So I wait. Nevertheless, it isn't easy being bombarded with messages that I can't respond to.

So I mostly spend my day getting ready for my dinner with Dave. Dave has made me forget everything. The idea of his arms, his touch, his laugh, finding him at last. He's like hot chocolate for the soul.

Agh, I'm being so cheesy. Dave makes me cheesy.

I take a bath, shave, give myself a face mask, choose an outfit that's cute but not too cute — jean skirt and loose T-shirt tucked in — go out and buy some wine, pay my credit card bill, pluck my eyebrows, clip my toenails, moisturize my legs so they're super soft, take my time putting on my makeup but not too early so I'll still have an angel face for cocktails.

In short, I am ready.

I sit on my speckled pastel two-seater waiting patiently for Dave to give me some sign of life. I especially don't want to look needy or, worse, like someone who eats too early.

I hold out until 6:20 p.m. before I break down and go back on the promise I made myself not to be the one who texts first.

E: About what time did we say? Can I bring anything?

Opale and Alice have gone to an art-performance party. I watch the documentary on serial killers. I started from the beginning and got to the episode about the Black Widow of Connecticut, a woman who assassinates her husbands so she can get their life insurance but who is caught red-handed when she tries to electrocute her Romeo in the conjugal hot tub.

At 7:18 p.m., I redo my lipstick twice. My tights are itching me, they stick to the sofa fabric when I move, and it's annoying.

E: Houston, do you read me? :)

Friendly, but efficient.

Two endless minutes pass. Then my phone lights up, vibrates at last.

It's him.

D: Quinoa, I'm sorry.

I calm down. He's sorry for being late. He's sorry for burning the lasagna. He's sorry for every second he has to spend away from me.

I wait. Nothing.

My fingers compose a friendly, charming reply. But my face would frighten a baby cat.

E: Tell me more, Mr. Lanctôt.

I wait.

D: It won't work tonight after all.

E: Ah, damn.

D: But we'll do it another time!

Oh, no. No . . . not the end of the world, not yet.
I take off my tights, toss them away and write:

E: No worries. I still have time to organize my spices.
I only got as far as fenugreek, so . . .

D: I apologize, I'm super disappointed.

He is disappointed, that's it.

D: I have to do the café closing all week, but could
we have lunch?

D: Are you tempted? Say yes! I know a place that
makes the best eggs benny in town.

Okay, so I have two questions. First, is tomorrow morning too soon? Second, is he going to tell me why he couldn't make it tonight or is that optional?

Doesn't matter, stay cool above all. Stay cool.

E: Yum. I'm available tomorrow morning or Tuesday.

E: Or whenever you want.

D: Perfect!

"Perfect," that's all. No day, no time, nothing to add to my calendar app.

I drop my phone on the pallet coffee table, stretch out on my lovely speckled pastel, stare at the ceiling. The minutes tick painfully by. I study the cracks, the molding, the light fixture. Cartography of a plaster ceiling.

I ask myself how I got here. All alone, my heart broken, the end of my nose freezing cold, in the process of developing a strange and intimate relationship with a couch.

Seems like this was not the plan. I wanted to listen to myself. I mean, this cannot be what it means to follow one's heart. There's something I didn't get, something I did not do well.

I close my eyes, concentrate, try to listen to my little inner voice.

Radio silence.

I feel empty, like an aboveground pool in the month of November. I pray for a sign, a bit of clarity.

What is happening? What do I need to do?

I wait, and then I have a feeling, an intuition.

I need to talk to Denise the cosmetician. Denise will know what to do.

30

8:02 p.m. I jump into a taxi. I try to remember what day and time it was when I last saw Denise. I try to gauge what my chances are of arriving during her shift. It was the evening just before I had dinner with my father, the night I first told him about my book. Sam had just let me down. She helped fix my makeup but most of all, she gave me an unforgettable pep talk. It's thanks to her that I had the courage to listen to my little inner voice. Without knowing it, this woman changed my life a little, and I need her tonight.

I pray during the long ride to the pharmacy that she'll be there behind her melamine counter, her hands full of samples, ready to dish out a truth that will shake me up but do me good.

I need you, Denise.

The driver drops me in front of the pharmacy. I dash across the sidewalk, push open the automatic door to make it open faster, go through the turnstile…

And there she is, my life coach, wearing a white blouse.

She's there, and she's not busy. She's waiting, waiting for me.

Thank you, life.

I go down the cosmetics aisle and stop in front of her, look at her. She's smaller than I remember.

I take a deep breath. Amazed, I don't take my eyes off her.

"Hello, Denise."

"Can I help you with something?"

Good. Okay, so I had considered that she might not recognize me, but I didn't consider it for long. I have to improvise.

"I'm looking for a good concealer…a very good concealer!"

"What is your budget?"

"No budget." Oops, no. I'm exaggerating. "Well, let's say around thirty dollars."

Denise nods, goes over to the PURE display — clearly her favorite — and chooses two small bottles and a sponge, motions for me to sit down in her padded chair.

I am overjoyed. I hold my breath.

"I'll start by trying you on the medium coverage," she says. "And after that I'll show you the full coverage."

"Super!"

While she applies a bit of magic beneath my eyes,

I tell myself that I have no choice but to go straight to the heart of the matter. The last time, I was sad, and she understood that I needed help. Now it's not so clear.

I'll ask her a question. It's bold, but I didn't come here just to leave with concealer. I have at least fifteen unopened tubes at home.

I try to formulate a question, maybe something like, So, Denise, how do you know which one of your little voices is *the* little voice? Because I am really confused and I don't know any more whether the voice I'm listening to is the one that makes good decisions or the…

But she stops suddenly, takes a step back, puts her fist on her hip.

"Hold on a second, you look familiar."

She looks at me. Digs into her memory. My eyes are saying, "It's me, Denise! You put cherry red lipstick on my lips, do you remember?" I see an excited look in her eyes. Something has clicked in her head. A big click, because she turns on her little heels and goes to the front of the store.

"Yes, yes, yes, it's you! Don't move!"

I find it weird, but I wait, I leave things to her.

She returns with her feet drumming on the floor, a magazine in her hand.

"It's you! You're that little singer's girlfriend, the gorgeous Samuel Vanier!"

Denise points to my photo on the cover of *Femme*. The big headline reads, "Ellie and Sam's Vegan Christmas." I had completely forgotten that it was already out. Completely.

"Oh, yes! It's me...it's me..." I stammer.

"Can I ask for your autograph?"

"Yes...of course, no prob —"

"No, but you have hit the big time with him. You are very lucky, my little brunette."

It looks like I'm going to leave here with some concealer and all my problems intact.

Thanks for nothing, God. Thanks for nothing.

31

Alice and I take turns sleeping at my father's. To keep an eye on him until he moves into the cottage for good. In the evenings, we organize pajama parties. Alice has suggested a marathon of movies from our childhood. She selected titles that we used to watch on our old DVD player every summer. Our classics.

Tonight we're starting with the *Alien* movies, my father's favorites. Next up it's *Indiana Jones.*

Tucked up in a fleece blanket, I watch Lieutenant Ellen Ripley and her team wake up in 2122 after a small nap in space that lasted for ten months.

I poke my phone every five minutes. I've hidden it under my blanket and turned the brightness down to minimum. Alice knows that I've been waiting to hear from Dave for two days, and I don't want her giving me her big eyes as she tells me to turn it off for the thousandth time.

I try to concentrate on the film. I watch helplessly as poor Officer Kane is about to have his entrails ripped open by a slug from outer space. Life is short. Who knows whether or not I'm two seconds away from having my insides crushed by some unknown life-form. Who knows?!

I've decided that I want to see Dave more than I want to look independent. Woman up, I tell myself.

I compose a message and press Send. Bam.

E: Going out for bennies tomorrow? I've had a hankering ever since you mentioned it.

I immediately regret it. See what I've just done. I have no game, I so don't have game. A bit out of desperation, I distractedly watch the crew trying to get their hands on the extraterrestrial that is running rampant in their outer space tent trailer when I finally receive a reply.

D: I have a meeting at the beginning of the day, but we could maybe go before? I don't know, around 7? They have an early-bird special.

An early-bird special. A date at 7:00 in the morning. What?

I hesitate. Is this his way of telling me he's not interested, or is it really impossible for him to see me any other time? And, like, if I accept, do I look like a girl who's desperate or a girl who's easygoing?

I give myself five minutes to think about it. But YOLO. I listen to my heart.

E: Sure! Why not. What restaurant were you thinking of?

We finish the first movie and then we watch the second one, where even in 2179, poor Ellen Ripley is still at war in the far reaches of the galaxy with a band of marines armed to the teeth.

Toward the end, my father falls asleep in his armchair. His mouth open, his neck bent. Poor Papa. Soon he'll need full-time help. Soon...I don't want to think about it.

With Alice, I help him get to bed. I kiss his forehead, feel his warm, sour breath.

"I'm not such a big deal anymore, eh, cocopomme?" he says.

It upsets me to see him like this. He's shivering, I wrap him in his duvet, put a second pair of socks on him, lie down beside him to help warm him up. I watch his face, I watch him fall asleep, I get myself used to our intimacy at the same time as I get used to the idea of him leaving.

Back in the living room, I stop the film to give the indefatigable Ellen Ripley a break. I replace the cushions on the couch, find my phone in my blanket and realize that even in 2179, Dave has not replied.

32

Mother-daughter yoga. The class ended ten minutes ago. I wait in the locker room for my little yellowy-orange mother to leave the studio. To come and take her shower. She's taking a long time, so I go back to the studio and find her asleep on her mat. She's sleeping with her mouth open.

It's embarrassing. I wake her up.

"No..." she says, confused. "Just another minute."

"Maman! The sun is shining, the birds are singing, and you fell asleep during Savasana. Get up!"

It reminds me of the days when my mother would follow the latest fad diet — South Beach, Atkins, Master Cleanse — and walked around looking like a very well dressed but vaguely hypoglycemic zombie. Anyone who thinks my diets are intense has never seen my mother's. She doesn't go on them often now, but when she gets into it, it is something to behold. I imagine that she didn't like seeing herself in a bathing suit in Mexico. It depresses me. I hope I won't be like that at her age. At the same time, I seem to be walking straight into that particular wall.

I help her get up, a little annoyed. I have enough

problems as it is, I'd really rather not have to deal with any more.

She stretches, sniffs.

"It smells like your grandmother's meat sauce in here," she says. "Don't you think?"

I take her hand.

"Come on, Maman," I say, speaking slowly. "I have a granola bar in my bag."

33

"Sam, I don't have time for your bullshit."

"It's not bullshit, just listen to me for one minute. Please."

"Nope. We'll do the shoot, and then I'm leaving."

I had no choice but to honor a contract that I signed last month in anticipation of the holidays. A photo for Bulles de France of me toasting in the new year while eating cake in my kitchen with Sam.

I slide two champagne flutes on the counter.

"These are the glasses the client approved," I say.

"Ellie! I did not sleep with Mila after your launch."

"I don't give a shit."

"She's the one who kissed me!"

"Don't care."

I start to unwrap the layer cake that I bought in the fancy little pastry shop that serves good coffee. I was supposed to bake one myself, but I'd rather spend the time with my father. I lift off the original garnish of edible flowers and replace it with sprigs of rosemary. No one will be the wiser. I lift the cake out of the box and place it on a marble cake stand. Just like in the mood board that I sent the client.

Sam takes off his T-shirt and puts on the shirt I laid out for him.

"When Mila found out we weren't together any-more, she became very intense."

"Wait, what? Mila knows? She's known since the beginning?"

"Yeah...We texted."

"Fun."

"She's the one who started to DM me first."

"When?"

"During my tour. My gig in Minneapolis."

The information slowly seeps into my brain, pricks my gray matter one cell at a time. My knees buckle when I understand that while she and I were spending the evening together at the Anti-Bullying Gala, while we were shooting videos together and making travel plans — all that time Mila was happily texting my boyfriend.

"You've been exchanging messages for a month?"

"More or less."

"What kind of messages?"

"It depends. At first we were just chatting. Then at some point...it got more serious...We sent photos and stuff."

"Photos...so between a couple of selfies of your-selves in underpants, you told her about our breakup."

"I didn't have anyone to talk to about it! It was huge for me."

"And you never slept together. Really?"

"Okay...Once. She came here one night, this was before your launch, you were at Alice's, we weren't together anymore."

This hurts me so much.

"And how was it?" I ask, my heart in shreds.

I need details to torture myself with, to imprint the pain. I want to know. I need to know.

"Did you like it?"

"No. I'm not going to talk about that."

"It was nicer than with me?"

"Ellie..."

I imagine them having sex in our bed. Tell myself that they must have looked beautiful naked. That they go well together. I feel like garbage, and realize that Sam slept with Mila even before the photos of the two of them in the bar began to circulate on the internet.

I didn't see any of this coming when Mila was pre-tending to be my friend. I saw nothing.

The anger rises up to strangle me. It's violent.

"So the fact is that at the launch, when you came to help me during my panic attack, you were already sleeping together! Fuck, you must have been dying with laughter, I can't believe it. Then all the nice things you said to me were fucking bullshit!"

"No! Everything I said to you was true!"

"So why did you sleep with her in the first place? Of all the people in the world, I can't believe that you chose Mila fucking Mongeau."

"But what about you! You're the one who left! You left me, you cheated on me, you fell in love with someone else! It's you, Ellie. It's not me...So don't come and lecture me."

"But it hurts me, Sam."

"Me too. I haven't stopped hurting, not for one second since you left. Not for a second!...Not one!"

I lower my head, I'm devastated. I'm like a three-year-old child. I want some adult to come and find me. Put my heart back together one piece at a time.

Sam can tell.

"After your launch," he says softly, "I knew it was over with Mila, that I was going to wait for you."

"Are you kidding me? You kissed her."

"She tricked me!"

"Oh, really! You can't tell me that —"

"No, listen! After the launch, Mila texted to check on me. I was sad, you'd left. She invited me to go out for a drink, and I accepted, telling her that it would just be as friends…Then she kissed me. I didn't see it coming, I never thought she would do that in a public place, she knew it was a secret, and how it was super important and everything."

"Do you really think I'm going to believe that, that your affair wasn't planned? You knew that people would see you together in the bar, that it wasn't just harmless."

He shrugs but doesn't say anything. Instead, he takes out his camera, fiddles with it, adjusts the settings. I find it arrogant.

"Okay, maybe I liked the idea of getting a reaction out of you."

"For revenge?"

"Because I don't give a shit about Mila. You're the one I want on my team, Ellie, and I'm going to wait for you. I am waiting for you."

I can't deny that hearing him say that gives me some satisfaction.

"You're annoying."

He smiles with the corners of his lips. I watch him set the camera on the tripod, doesn't take his eyes off it. I'm surprised to find him handsome in his shirt, desirable. He can tell. I'm not particularly subtle.

"Are you still seeing the little guy with the mustache who draws hearts on café au laits?"

"No."

"I thought you were 'in love'..."

"Yeah, well, I was mistaken. He's not...It wasn't... I made a big mistake."

"I guess that goes for both of us."

Sam smiles sadly. It's like we're looking into each other's souls. I shrug my shoulders.

I'm sad. So sad. He gives me one of his irresistible smiles, that makes him look like a little kitten but more manly. My favorite. I feel a kind of sweet drunkenness come over me when he comes closer, puts his hand on my cheek, looks at my lips.

I smile, grip the counter, close my eyes, feel his body against mine. We kiss, I like it, I like it a lot. I slip back into my old life like a worn T-shirt straight out of the dryer. Find those fresh but familiar feelings again. It is so nice, so soothing. I realize what I almost lost.

"I'm sorry," I say, looking down at the ground.

He takes my chin, lifts it up, forces me to look at him.

"Do you love me?" he asks.

And that's when I have an idea, a great idea. I give in to it.

"How would you like to take a trip to New Zealand?" I ask.

34

Before I know it, it's already the middle of December. I feel better, much better. My book is launched, I've got some nice contracts, a wedding to organize, and I have quietly rediscovered my new-old life with Sam. No more sleeping on the speckled pastel two-seater couch for me. I'm sleeping in my own bed, except I have to spend time at the cottage with my father. His condition is stable since he went back to the place he loves most in the world, since he's had a medical team looking after him. I'm going to go and see him as often as possible.

But not today. Today I have a check-in meeting with Malik and Mila.

So, what's happening, basically, is that I convinced the VP of Banana Apparel that the New Zealand trip could happen very well without Mila. I would go with Sam instead.

Needless to say, I've not been looking forward to coming to the agency to face Mila and explain why I've stolen her part of the trip after she tried to steal my boyfriend. It seems to me there's nothing else to say. I would appreciate it if she had the class not to make a big deal about it, but apparently it's turned into a huge drama. She's not just leaving it for Malik to deal with. That's why he insisted on the two of us meeting with him. To discuss it.

When I go into the office, she's sitting down, her arms crossed, wearing dark glasses. It's already so dramatic, I almost want to laugh. If she saw what real-life drama looks like — helping your sick father wipe his bottom after he goes to the bathroom — she might understand that she's acting like a big baby.

I sit down in the chair beside her. Wait for Malik to start talking.

But when he opens his mouth, Mila cuts him off instantly, talks like she's been holding her breath for ten minutes.

"What right do you have to renegotiate my project with Banana Apparel without telling me?"

Her tone irritates me. I look at Malik as witness, answer her in a reasonable voice.

"We were not going to go together after you were seen kissing my fiancé. It wasn't going to work."

"You could have pulled out of the project."

"Sure, but...I don't know what to tell you...they were happy at Banana when I suggested that Sam could take your place, like really. I didn't even have to convince them . . ."

"Ellie, this trip, the festival, was my idea! I organized the whole thing, it's my dream, not yours! What right do you have?"

"Yeah, and Sam is my boyfriend, not yours, but that didn't stop you from sleeping with him."

I look at Malik with big eyes, trying to read his thoughts, waiting for him to say something in my defense. He looks a bit out of his depth. I'm aware that what I did isn't totally right, but I think the payback is fair. I'll take over her project, and then we'll all move on to other things. A trip would do me good after the fall I've just had. I'm sure Malik agrees. He just can't say it.

Mila collects her thoughts, makes an effort to look friendly and measured.

"I know you blame me, Ellie, but —"

"I don't blame you, Mila."

And that's true. I hate her, but I don't blame her. If I have managed to forgive Sam, I should do the same thing for her . . . and I'm working on it. In any case, given the messages she's receiving right now, I wouldn't want to be in her shoes. People are accusing her of coming between Sam and me. Of trying to seduce him, of sabotaging our relationship. And they think we were best friends, which makes it even worse.

She's taking the blame, as if it's her fault and not Sam's. I find the relentless attacks on her shocking. She doesn't deserve that. I don't understand why Sam doesn't get the same treatment. He's gotten a few messages, but that's all. Anyway, it's no one else's business.

"I would have liked for us to be friends," I add. "I tried. I meant it, but I don't think it's possible for the two of us. We've got too much baggage. You were right about that from the beginning."

She wants to say something. She opens her mouth, but has nothing to add. I look at her with compassion as she wipes her tears behind her big dark glasses.

I've been waiting for this moment for a long time, and I'm enjoying every second.

"No hard feelings?" I say.

She shakes her head, collects her things, leaves the office.

I've won. We're done.

I turn to Malik.

"So, no news about my leggings collection yet?"

Top 10 YouTubers CAN/FR

1. Jordanne Jacques – 810,000 followers
2. Tellement Cloé – 765,000 followers
3. **Ellie – Quinoa Forever – 505,000 followers**
4. **Cath Bonenfant – 504,000 followers**
5. Mila Mongeau – 501,000 followers
6. Emma & Juju – 497,000 followers
7. Approved by Gwen – 429,000 followers
8. Sophie Chen – 346,000 followers
9. Maëla Djeb – 167,000 followers
10. Zoé around the World – 149,000 followers

CELEBRITY WORLD

Pleading exhaustion, Mila Mongeau takes a break from social media

Mila Mongeau knows social media like the back of her hand. And while she has largely benefitted from it over the past years, she has recently suffered setbacks. On Sunday she wrote an Instagram post to say that she would be quitting social media until Christmas in order to "reconnect with herself." Read her message here . . .

Élisabeth Bourdon-Marois and Samuel Vanasse pick a wedding date!

In a post that's both cute and touching, the lovers unveiled a photo of the enchanting vineyard where their wedding will take place next summer. Though they remain evasive about the exact date, we at least know that the celebrations will take place sometime between Saint-Jean-Baptiste and Labor Day . . .

Selena St-Aubin on the Seb Hadiba affair: "I'm angry"

Last night, Selena St-Aubin was at *Just Chatting* to discuss the third season of *Singles* and to comment on the Seb

Hadiba case, which has required Seb to apologize publicly barely a month after being targeted by allegations of sexual assault . . .

35

Tomorrow is Christmas. My father's last. My sister and I have promised each other that it won't be sad. We gave his caregivers time off, and we decided to hunker down at the cottage for the most beautiful family reunion ever. My mother and Nico arrived this morning, and they're taking the room on the second floor. My father and his medical equipment are in the ground-floor bedroom. Opale and Alice are taking the fold-out couch in the living room. Sam and I are on an inflatable mattress in the hall — the luxury accommodation.

When everyone is there, the cottage becomes tiny. The windows are foggy, it smells like wood-smoke, old coffee and afternoon toast. We're warmed by our own company, don't even need to dress like marshmallows.

It's not big inside, but outside it is. Outside it's huge. The river stretching into the distance. The ice drifting slowly, gently. From time to time the sky disappears when the wind blows the snow around in crazy gusts. Other times the sky is heavy and cottony all day long, until rays of sunlight stream through like a blessing. Some evenings it turns all pink, like a golden light show.

There is nowhere more beautiful than here. I feel good here.

While Nico and my mother have a nap (at least, I hope that's what they're doing), and Alice, Opale and my father play Risk, I cook with Sam. I've promised to honor the family tradition. Not Ellie and Sam's Vegan Christmas. No fake cheese, no watercress soup or roasted lentils. I'm making meatball stew, tourtière, turkey roll, mashed potatoes and an eggnog Yule log cake. It makes me happy.

Sam peels potatoes at the kitchen counter. He's smiling — the potatoes make him smile. I'm making the pastry for the tourtière. Right next to us in the dining room, Opale accuses Alice of cheating on her promise of peace in Kamchatka, one of the places on the game board. It's an oratorical joust of grand proportions:

"Op, the only person who's to blame here is you, for being so naive. Alliances are made to be broken. Only losers keep their word, everyone knows that."

"False! Completely false! Name me a single defector country that has been on the winning side of a major war."

"Easy. Italy during the First World War."

"Italy changed sides before the war, not during."

"If you want peace, prepare for war. Loser."

It's fascinating how seriously they take this.

"Loser yourself," Opale says. "Here's to world peace, asshole."

"Anyway, I'm not talking to players who don't control at least one continent."

"I have Australia!"

"Inconsequential continents don't count."

My father seems to be having a great time. He laughs, passes the dice to Opale.

"Here, roll your dice, Valentin Bulgakov."

"Papa, no," Alice says. "Don't start with the obscure Russian references in front of Opale…"

"The only thing that's obscure is ignorance! Bulgakov was Tolstoy's secretary, and he was also…"

I'm listening to them distractedly while rolling out my pastry, and I realize that Sam is looking at me out of the corner of his eye.

"What?"

He shakes his head. Wipes his hands on his apron, runs his tongue over his lips, his fingers through his hair. He looks straight into my eyes.

"What is it?" I ask again.

"Nothing, nothing."

"Sam, stop fooling around! What?"

I give him a little hip bump. He turns to me, takes my hand, his eyes shining, piercing right through me. He kneels down in front of me.

I melt, and crouch down with him. Hidden behind the island, we are alone in the world.

"I've been thinking a lot lately," he whispers. "I don't want to be a big cliché, Ellie. I want to become a better person for you, to be your person."

I take his face in my hands.

"I'm interested," I say, moved. "Very."

"Élisabeth Bourdon-Marois, will you marry me?"

The sun is shining golden rays on the kitchen floor. I take a deep breath. I never thought I could feel like this, after everything that has happened. To feel in love.

"Yes, I will."

This time, I mean it, completely. I hug him.

We aren't perfect, but I want to take the risk. I'm all in. We look at each other, happy. Normally he would put a ring on my finger, but I'm already wearing his ring. The show must go on. We've picked a date, reserved the vineyard, I've even put a deposit on a dress. It reassures me that he's taking the time to do things right. It gives me hope — hope that the autumn we've been through was just a detour on our way.

I'm letting myself be carried by the river, a small block of drifting ice, ready to go wherever.

Sam gets up, pulls me to him, grabs me by the waist.

We keep kissing, I'm floating.

"Get a room!" I hear Alice yell.

Easier said than done.

36

Dinner is almost ready. Alice takes care of the salad while I change in the bathroom. I keep on my big wool socks, put on a dress. The dress with the gold sequins. It was too small at the Karma Christmas dinner. I hope it will fit me now.

I think about Beyoncé in her documentary *Homecoming*. The one where you see her preparing for her big comeback at Coachella. Where she rehearses tirelessly to put on her show, get her body back after having twins. I remember the emotion on her face when she managed to put on her old stage costume. She thought she'd never be able to get into it. I remember her joy when she talked about all the sacrifices she'd had to make to get there, when she said, "I'm back in my costume. It zipped!"

I would like to feel like her.

I suck in my stomach, hold my breath, put on the dress, pull the zipper.

It fits. I contemplate my reflection in the mirror. I look at my profile, put on a smile for the camera.

I did it. The dress, the top three, I achieved my goals.

I'm back in my costume.

37

I take the tourtière out of the oven, place it on the table, watch my mother dig in to her plate of mashed potatoes and meatball stew like there's no tomorrow.

Long live Christmas.

I sit at the table between Sam and my father, across from Alice. I propose a toast to my father, to the family.

I raise my wine-glass, look at each of the people sitting around the table. I love them. This is a lot better than the last time. Our real Christmas beats the Karma Christmas by a long shot.

My father goes to speak. He takes his time, but still runs out of breath.

"Thank you all for being here. An official welcome ... to our new members — Opale, Nicolas, Samuel — you are here with us ... in our family. Alice, Élisabeth, Estelle ... nothing pleases me more ... than your happiness ... to see you happy. You are ... the light at the end of my tunnel."

My father is beautiful. I rub his back, kiss his cheek, start to eat the pointy part of my tourtière, a knot in my throat. I take a few bites of turkey, try to follow the conversations without losing control and weeping into my potatoes. I listen to Sam talking to Opale about famous serial killers, but I'm just con-centrating on my plate.

I've eaten too much. I throw my napkin on my plate so I won't be able to touch it. I'm tired — tired of limits, tired of keeping an eye on myself. I want to enjoy life without thinking about it.

Nico takes advantage of the silence to raise his glass of mineral water.

"Estelle and I have some big news to announce."

Alice bursts out laughing, raises her glass of red like she's going to propose a toast, too. Her mouth is full of mashed-up meat and tomato chutney.

"Maman is pregnant!" she says.

This is clearly not her first glass of wine. I think she's being insensitive. It's not funny anyway. But that's Alice for you. No tact.

To my great surprise, Nico answers, "Yes. That's exactly it. We're expecting a baby."

The silence that follows is one of the strangest that I've ever experienced. I get the impression that everyone wants to say something nice, but it's like we're paralyzed with an astonishment and awkward-ness that is difficult to hide.

Everyone except Opale.

"You're going to adopt?" she asks.

My mother laughs, savoring the moment, relishes each word that she says.

"No, I'm pregnant! It's still early days, and of course we have to get through the first trimester, but the results of the latest ultrasound are very encouraging. If everything goes as planned, we'll be giving birth in July."

She's proud, it seems. Proud to be pregnant at the age of forty-nine and a half. It's a provocation, a kick in the teeth to the established order. My mother is a teenager.

"We heard two hearts during the ultrasound!" Nico adds, beaming. "Two hearts!"

"Twins," Opale exclaims. "Oh, too cool, congratulations! Alice, you're going to be an aunt!"

My father clears his throat.

"Big sister," he clarifies.

"Big sister, I mean!"

What the...what? I'm stunned. My mother calls out to Nico who's sitting across from her. She calls him "mi cielo," and holds out her small hand to him across the table. Nico does the same, and they have to stretch to touch each other with their fingertips. They gaze at each other like God and Adam on the ceiling of the Sistine Chapel. My mother is radiant. It seems everything has gone exactly the way she planned. Nico whispers that he loves her.

"I'm very happy for you both," my father says solemnly at the other end of the table. "I hope to still be of this world, to be able to hold your little ones. Boys or girls, do you know?"

"Not yet!"

I am...what? I'm chewing the inside of my cheek. My mother is expecting twins. She is going to create life while my father is losing his.

Am I the only one struck by the irony of this situation? It's indecent, no?

"Not that I want to get into the details," I say. "But did this...happen by accident or..."

My mother laughs loudly. Her good mood irritates me. She's like a party hat at a funeral.

"No," she replies. "At my age, you don't get pregnant by accident. We went to a fertility clinic in Mexico. The waiting list is too long here. Nico and I have no time to lose."

In Mexico. The backpacking trip. The self-tanning

lotion, falling asleep in yoga, the enormous appetite. I can't believe it.

"Having a child is a dream that we've cherished ever since we confessed our feelings for each other," she continues.

I do the math in my head, figure out that she's been cherishing this dream for less than three months, which might as well be two seconds.

Nico's eyes are brimming. Clearly this is a subject that moves him a great deal.

"I've always wanted to be a father. For me, there was no doubt when I met Estelle that she was going to be the mother of my children."

Sam chokes on his glass of water. I give him a kick under the table. I get the feeling this is a big deal for Nico. Something momentous. He's going to be a father, and probably a good one.

I let myself soften. A little. However, I don't manage to put my feelings into words. Neither does Alice.

It's Opale who has the conversation with my mother.

"I think it's wonderful that you two are taking the liberty to do exactly what you want, without worrying about what other people might think. That takes courage."

"Exactly. I feel like the timing is ideal for us. I'm trusting in my intuition, and in Nicolas, too."

The way she says "Nicolas," drawing out the A. I see Opale give Alice a little nudge to encourage her to say something.

"Well, yes, Estelle," my sister says. "Retirement is considered to be the ideal time to have children."

She takes her plate and starts to clear the table.

My mother is ready.

"Why not? I had you at a time in my life when you had to be a mother and have a career as well, reclaim your body, succeed as a couple — all at the same time. That didn't work out so well for me. This time it will be different. I will have time to cherish our little cariños."

Sam gets up to do the dishes with Alice. Taking my mother's plate, he says, "Anyway, it's super. It will give us a chance to look after them and practice before it's our turn, won't it, bunny?"

He looks at me, and I give him A for effort.

"I think it's pretty badass," Opale adds. "I am full of admiration."

I excuse myself politely, leave the table, say that I'm going out to get some air, that I've eaten too much. Sam asks if I'm okay, and I say yes. I put on my boots, my coat.

Opale is right. My mother is taking the liberty of doing exactly what she wants, and that bothers me.

It bothers me deeply.

38

I walk out into the darkness of the back balcony, swipe the snow off a lawn chair with my forearm, sit down and sulk.

I hear the patio door open and close. Opale appears. She puts down her glass of wine in the snow and rummages around in her pockets.

"We miss you at the apartment. Maya left her boyfriend, but it's funny, I still feel like someone's missing."

I smile. It makes me happy to hear that. In a weird way, I also feel a bit nostalgic about my "walking wounded" phase.

"Yeah, I didn't think I would ever say this, but I even miss my old friend the speckled pastel couch, and your ugly face."

"So if I convince Alice to let me move in to her room with her, you could take mine. You like it, don't you?"

She takes out a pack of cigarettes and slides one between her lips, finds a lighter and lights it.

"A cigarette? Yuck!"

"That's what your sister thinks, too, but it's

Christmas. I'm indulging myself."

"That's what I told myself earlier when I had a glass of eggnog, but I regret it now."

"So what exactly is the problem with eggnog?"

Opale takes a puff of her cigarette, blows out the smoke. I watch the little gray cloud waltz away.

"Think about it," I say. "It's a punch made with eggs. It's disgusting."

"What, are you kidding me?"

"No, but I'm not going to have another glass. I forget every year! I forget that I didn't like it the year before ... I need to make a note in my calendar app to remind me that —"

"You're mad at your mother?"

"Oh. That."

She picks up her glass from the snow and takes a sip. I try to gather my thoughts. Wrap them up in some pretty paper to make them presentable.

"She could have waited until ... having twins, at her age! Before my ... It's ridi ..."

I sigh. My breath spills out into the cold air.

"She's acting like there are no rules! She's doing exactly what she wants. And it bugs me. A lot."

"You don't do what you want?"

"No, nobody does what they want! That's not the way things work."

"I wouldn't say that."

My fingers are freezing, and I tuck them into my sleeve to warm them.

"Why do you do this?" I ask. "Why do you always come to help me?"

"I don't know. You remind me of my sister."

"You have a sister?"

"Agathe. You remind me of her. She's also had an eating disorder since...forever."

This shakes me. I want to protest, but I stay calm.

"You think I have an eating disorder?"

"I don't know. Honestly, I don't know. Maybe."

I make an effort not to say anything. To let it drop.

My eyes are gradually getting used to the dark.

"I don't know..." I say. "As twisted as this might sound, watching my weight helps me deal with myself. If I don't feel good, if I don't achieve my goal or if someone doesn't like me, I tell myself it's my fault. That it's because of my weight. It's simpler, and I have power over it. I can deal with that. A diet, a food plan, a new 'lifestyle.' I don't know about all the rest of it."

Opale tilts her head back to think, takes a deep breath, exhales, straightens.

"I apologize for the unsolicited advice," she says, "but I don't understand why you keep doing that. Your career, the whole thing...clearly it's not helping you. It's not making you happy."

"Nothing will make me happy."

She shrugs. "I still don't think it's the only option."

"There are lots of people who manage to be happy in this business!"

"Yeah, sure...but not you. I've seen the way you are, and it's not exactly working out for you."

I start to be able to see the river in the dark. A thick chunk of ice on the bank. The little frozen mountains.

I'm cold.

As if she guesses as much, Opale leans over and gives me a hug, holding her cigarette as far away as possible. I lean my head on her shoulder. Bury my face in her coat, which stinks.

"I grew up thinking I was broken," I say. "That I needed to fix myself, and I've never stopped trying."

"Maybe you've never been broken," Opale suggests softly. "Maybe you also have the right to do exactly what you want."

I sit there frozen. It seems like a revolutionary idea. I think about it. It scares me.

"You're an asshole, but I love you, Op. Alice is crazy not to want to be your girlfriend."

She laughs, a laugh without joy.

"You should tell her that," she says.

"No, you should tell her that! That not being a couple is not okay with you. Because that's the way you feel, right?"

"Yes."

"Tell her! That's my unsolicited advice. That and quit smoking."

She takes one last puff of cigarette. Leans over to put it out in the snow, in the little circle left by her glass. She gets up and looks away.

"I can't do that. I don't want to lose her."

"At worst, you can come and sleep on my couch."

"Your five-thousand-dollar sofa? No, thanks. It's hideous."

I smile. Her big old turtle shell is never far away.

"You're hideous!"

"I've created a monster."

"I also have an inflatable mattress. Thirty bucks at a garage sale."

"Tempting."

"It smells a bit like stale cigarettes. Should remind you of your room."

"Excuse me! What are you talking about? My bed smells great!"

"Anyway, if Alice breaks up with you, I guess I'll just have to beat the crap out of her."

SELF-LOVE

I wish I could say I've learned to love myself the way I am. That would be nice, it would sound good, a happy ending. To say that I'm perfectly imperfect, and that's perfect. That I learned to love myself the way no one has before. That I have made peace with the body that made me invisible, excluded, despised, ashamed. Tell a story of self-love. A beautiful story, something that would give hope, something "authentic." To say, "This is my journey, you guys! This is me! I've finally figured it out!"

But...no. I can't do it. I have no choice but to tell it like it is. To say that I am still afraid of my body. Afraid of what it once was and what it could become.

I am full of contradictions. I'm horrified by the culture that put me on a diet at the age of ten, that still makes me feel like a failure every day, at every meal. The culture that always puts me in front of my mirror, never truly alive, never facing the world. I hate it. But I also carry it inside me, and freeing myself from it is an imperfect process. My body isn't a shield or armor. I don't dress it up in fuck yous, like a provocation. My body is a wound that I'm trying to heal. That I reopen often.

I want to be loved, too. I navigate between two narratives — between two poles. To love myself, to change myself. I've built one part of me to disguise the other part. Ellie who stands in front of Élisabeth. I don't even know which is the true one, the good me.

Which one is "me"? The one that feels broken, or the one who wants to fix it? Which of the two am I?

Maybe this is my story, that I will never live up to those standards, or be able to love myself without them. Between the girl that I think I am and the one I want to be, there's a little gap. Today I understand that I will never be one or the other. That I will always exist somewhere between the two.

39

Tomorrow, Sam and I are flying to New Zealand.

I help my father get into bed. I won't see him for two whole weeks.

He sits on the edge of his bed. I turn on his electric blanket, lift his legs to help him pivot onto the bed.

He stops me.

"I'm not strong, either," he says.

I look at him, confused.

"When we were at the apartment, you said that... you would have wished that... I had taught you how to be independent and strong... like me. I'm sorry to disappoint you, my love... but I think... you're mistaken."

His eyes are bright, he swallows with difficulty.

"If I didn't teach you how to be free, it's... because I didn't know... how to do it... myself. I'm like you, Élisabeth... in search of the ideal. I've played my whole life at... being strong. I was afraid... of never being enough... never being big enough. And look at me now... Tragic irony."

I have a hard time believing him. It doesn't seem possible.

"But your mother ... I think your mother is in the middle of ... understanding something important. She's the one who ... can give you ... a lesson or two in that department."

I'm stunned. He's right. He's right.

"I don't know if I want to be like her ..." I murmur.

He smiles, a sad smile.

I take his hand.

"When I come back," I say, "we need to play Scrabble again. I haven't had a chance to beat you yet."

"Impossible. I am unbeatable."

"Not so much anymore."

He starts to smile. "That's enough of that, my girl. A little respect for your old man."

I laugh until silence overwhelms us.

"How do you do it, Papa? How do you keep laughing?"

His little eyes are like a misty sky. He takes a long time to answer.

"When I think that I'm going to sink ... into a kind of madness ... I try to remember that life ... owes me nothing. I'm the one that owes everything to it ... I'm letting it ... strip me of everything it has given me. I'm letting it take me."

I clutch his hand, as if that could stop him from leaving. From drifting away to his other place.

I have only just learned how to love you. I am just starting to understand that I am like you. I'm with you, Papa, I am your rock. Stay, stay a bit longer.

David Lanctôt has sent you a message

D: Hey what's up Quinoa?

E: I don't know. The NASDAQ?

D: A stock market joke! Wow, I like it. More stock market jokes.

D: I thought of you while I was eating pretzels. Do you have plans tonight?

E: Are you serious?

D: Very. Pizza?

E: I am available between 5:50 p.m. and 6:10 p.m.

D: Huh?

D: Ellie?

D: Hello? Are you there?

D: Earth to Ellie!

D: Hello?

19,009 Likes

ellie_quinoa_forever At the dawn of the new year, **@sam_van** and I will raise our glasses of **@bullesdefrance** to you, the beautiful community of Quinoa Forever. Thank you for being here!

Whoa, the year that's coming to an end makes me feel like I've been in a strange sort of chaos. It hasn't been easy, but I'm slowly learning to surround myself with people who are worth it. I make my way, I grow and I want to share my truth with you.

I wish you more kindness, more compassion, more listening . . . More love! More truth! I always make a wish on the night of the 31st, and that's what I wish for this year — truth, health and happiness! The year to come is looking wonderful. **#ad #happynewyear #sparklingwine**

See all 121 comments

gentardif You are my favorites, so beautiful.

sarah.love So glad you're still whole. Love is beautiful.

luciesimard Cheers to you both!

mimicriveau Awwwwww!

jessicaroy You are SO radiant!

hair.extensions You guys!

soso1997 Your words ring hollow forever.

elenaventura Happy New Year Ellie!

simone_sino WOW.

martinbazinet Very happy new year Ellie!

fabila_fleur HAPPY NEW YEAR LOVERS

vero2016 We love you.

mariejfrigon So inspiring!!!!

40

Sam puts our two huge suitcases in the trunk of the taxi. I greet the driver and get into the back seat. We're not late, but we're not early. It would only take a traffic jam to make us miss our first flight. That would be a catastrophe.

I think about everything that is to come — thirty hours of flying, two stopovers. First Toronto, then Hong Kong. I just hope they don't lose our baggage. Our outfits for Banana Apparel, our equipment.

I say a little prayer...

The car turns onto the highway, merges with traffic. I'm excited. I love airports, browsing through the magazine kiosks, the duty-free shop, traveling in the plane, landing, the border agents, the cold drinks, the hot meals, the little spots of turbulence that make me feel alive. I can't wait for it all.

I turn to Sam. His little morning eyes. I smile at him, happy we're together.

41

It's hot in the taxi, it smells like citrus fruit and anti-septic gel. The driver is listening to talk radio, and it's giving me a headache.

As always when I don't know what to do, I open an app on my phone, then another, and another. TikTok, photos, emails, Instagram — the possibilities are endless.

I am in "killing time" mode when an unusual comment on Instagram catches my attention. I always see the same keywords in the comments: "beautiful, wow, inspiring." I usually skim over them without really reading them.

But I spot the comment under my photo for Bulles de France right away. It stands out.

Divine Ludivine Shame on you!

Then I see another:

Yansa_D I am unfollowing this girl. Ciao bye!

And another:

Mirianne Boulay Hoping you apologized to Mila Mongeau for your actions before posting this. Kindness, my eye.

Mila Mongeau. What the ... I open her profile. Nothing special. I click on the link in her bio, get to her YouTube channel.

And I see it, the video with my name in the title: "I BREAK MY SILENCE ... ON MY FRIENDSHIP WITH ELLIE BOURDON-MAROIS."

It seems unreal. I open it. The video lasts for twenty-eight minutes.

Mila is not super well framed. No makeup, very poorly lit. She has done no editing.

I know right away that I'm in trouble.

I show the video to Sam. He freezes. I tell him that I'm going to watch, that he should do the same thing, and then we'll talk after.

I get out my earbuds, hold my breath and click Play.

The introduction goes on forever. She cries, talks about the past weeks, about the fact that she has reflected a lot, that she thinks it's important to establish the facts, that there are things that people need to know. She begins by admitting that, yes, she kissed Sam, but that it was just a tiny peck, a tipsy little accident.

"I'm so sorry! I am not proud of that, but I think everyone makes mistakes! I never wanted to hurt anyone! I didn't realize at the time, it happened so quickly, I didn't have time to think first. Doing something like this is completely unlike me, if you only knew! Bad timing, but Sam and I really had a great bond, it's hard to describe…"

She also explains that she's sad because she was supposed to fly to New Zealand today for a gig for Banana Apparel, something that has always been her dream, that everything had been organized, but that I stole her project away from her. That I used her work to get back at her.

The car is speeding in the fast lane. I sway from side to side. I feel sick, but I try to stay focused.

"The toxic relationship that Ellie and I have is not new. And I think I bear some of the responsibility for that." She points out that we have already been through a similar situation. To my amazement, she describes what happened to us in high school. Said she liked to "tease" me, that it "was not always nice," that I was jealous of her and that I sabotaged her most beautiful painting before the final exhibition. That to this day it remains one of the biggest traumas she has faced in her entire life.

"I think I have been lying to you for a long time. Ellie and I have never been friends."

In the taxi, the radio is too loud. I turn up my volume. My body takes on the rhythm of the road. I'm wobbly, I feel dizzy.

Then Mila says how our collaborations were essentially a strategy to profit from our mutual followers, to gain visibility. Confesses that she was reluctant at the beginning, but that she was convinced by her agent. "If I had to do it again, I would do otherwise. I have been doing a great deal of reflection work in these past weeks..."

I fast-forward the video, wonder what she could talk about for eighteen more minutes. I get to a part where she says that I do a lot of retouching on photos of my body. I start to panic, go back, listen to her explain that I am not the same person in real life as I am on the internet. "Ellie projects a certain image on her channel, and she's a girl who has lots of fine qualities, but I don't think you know her the way I know her..."

She leaves out nothing. She says I can be mean. That I am obsessed with my image. That things are not as perfect between Sam and me as people think. That I manipulate him, that he would do anything to make me happy.

I am in shock. She explains that when she kissed him in the bar, we were no longer together, that we'd split up. That she would never have approached him otherwise. Confides that in hindsight, she wonders whether she had developed real feelings for him.

Then she ends by asking her followers to forgive her for lying to them and says I should do the same thing.

I am glued to the screen of my phone. My mouth hanging open, I consider the smoking ruins of the image that I had so carefully constructed for myself. My brand image, the best version of myself. Now a little pile of hot, charred debris.

The car slows down, stops on the departure level. I turn to Sam, our faces like two kids in front of a horror movie.

He puts a hand in front of his mouth, says, "She texted me this morning. At the time I didn't understand. I didn't reply…"

He shakes his head vigorously, shows me the text that says, "I'm doing this for your own good XX."

"Oh...my...God. Sam. It's not just that she has it in for me. She's in love with you! She thinks she's saving you!"

#49 TRENDING

I BREAK MY SILENCE . . . ON MY FRIENDSHIP WITH ELLIE BOURDON-MAROIS

16,760 views • 2 hours ago

Mila Mongeau

503K subscribers

Hello YouTube! This video was very difficult for me to film. You were probably waiting for me to tell you about it . . . I am finally ready to reveal everything.

Thank you for your love and support!

Mila xxx

151 comments

Linda Lee

OMG OMG OMG OMG! I can't stop saying OMG! This story is HUGE.

SoSophie

Personally, I don't find it serious that you hid it from us, I understand! You are really strong we love you!!

Marina Gomez

Look, you don't have to apologize, Mimi! We are with you.

Amélie CB

Well no, unbelievable, I can't believe it, she seemed so nice!

Marie-Line Lemay

Thumbs up girl! Experiences, happy or not, make us grow.

Maëlle Dufour

Always knew that girl was FAKE. I'm unfollowing her.

See more

42

There's no time to lose. I go to the self-check-in while Sam frantically calls Malik. It rings and rings, but he does not pick up. Annoyed by how slow I am, Sam gently pushes me aside, takes control of the check-in, scans our passports, prints out our boarding passes and baggage tags. I stand beside him, lost, numb.

"Okay, I'm going to call Mila and ask her to pull the video. If I do it, she won't be able to say no."

"I think it's too late...it won't change anything. I have to explain myself, give my side of the story, we can tell people that...she's lying! That..."

I veer and get lost in the movement of the crowd. In the chaos of the airport, the frenzy of holiday vacationers.

Sam tries to be reassuring.

"We'll figure it out. We won't let it ruin your reputation. She doesn't know what she's got herself into."

"But how? We can't deny it. I...I did it. She may have come out of it ahead, and she takes a lot of liberties, but what she says is true. I sabotaged her painting, I took away her contract, I edited my photos...I mean, she's been clever! It pisses me off, but you have to hand it to her. She's fucking clever."

Is she right? Am I really that person? I can't believe it. I lose my composure, feel limp, like a wounded bird.

Sam thinks about it. Sighs, nods his head, clicks his tongue. He sticks big labels on our suitcases, takes my hand, pulls the suitcases with his other hand. Leads me to the baggage drop-off while speaking at top speed.

"We're going to expose her. I have a contact, a guy who works at *Narcisse*, Thomas. I'm positive we can find something on her, something that will make her look bad! He can publish it on their blog. It will be enough to plant doubt in people's minds. Make them see that she's not the person she pretends to be. Afterwards, we can give our side of things if you want. At that point, people will have good reason to believe you!"

"Okay, but what do we expose?"

"Well, let's say . . . It's no secret that Mila sleeps with . . . She told me things . . . Liam St-Pierre, he had just had a baby when . . ."

"Look, we can't do that! It's not our business . . . No!"

"Okay, okay. I'll think. Leave it to me."

He lifts our suitcases one at a time, puts them on the conveyor belt. I watch them move and disappear behind the curtain of plastic strips. Sam pulls me gently toward him by the strap of my little backpack and leads me to the security check with his arm around my shoulders. We pass a lot of people on the way, and I wonder whether they recognize me, whether they know. One guy holds my gaze a bit longer than normal... My heart is racing... Okay, I'm paranoid...

I calm down. It seems unreal at this moment, but it'll be all right. Everything will be okay. I do a breathing exercise that I learned in yoga — breathe in for four, hold my breath for four, breathe out for four.

I've been through worse. Everything is going to be okay.

The line to get through security is long, it's going to take forever. I decide to be brave and I go to check on the extent of the damage. YouTube, Instagram, *Celebrity World.*

I'm frightened. I'm afraid to look but I do anyway. I still hope some people will support me. That it won't be as bad as I imagine. That I can recover.

Mistake. Big mistake. It's a massacre.

It's violent. Truly. There are about two hundred mentions of the word "unfollow" in the comments under my photo for Bulles de France, but if that were only the end of it...

I have plenty of new messages.

miriannefmalo I am extremely disappointed to see at what point you became such a bitch nice example to set for young people

marcelchampagne Die whore.

johannepetris Have you considered seeing a psychologist about the fact that you use an app to change your body, it can be treated because at this point 99% of your intelligence is running down your thighs

karlbg You're so ugly even if I was your boyfriend I would like to fuck your best friend

And it goes on...for a long time. Next to this, my poutine story was a walk in the park. My eyes full of tears, I lock my phone, vowing not to touch it before I have a plan of action.

I glance at Sam, who is hooked to his phone like a climber to his carabiner. His knuckles white, his face tense. I can't stop thinking about Mila. I tell myself that she went through much the same thing a month ago with the comments, the messages...I couldn't imagine. Now I understand how much it hurts. For me it's been two seconds, but for her it lasted for way longer. I can't do it.

I'm praying for a miracle when Sam says, "Okay, I think I have it. I would rather find something else, but...I still have the messages — the text messages she sent me."

"What kind?"

"Compromising. Enough to deal with our problem. When they read them, people are going to understand that Mila is not at all the girl she pretends to be. When she says that she never wanted to hurt anyone, that what happened between her and me was just an accident, I have proof that it's false. She has completely contradicted herself. Look!"

He hands me his phone. I read, and it bothers me. A lot. I am stunned, but I'm still hesitating.

Is this really the thing to do? What will we look like afterwards?

I've scrolled to the bottom of the thread when my phone vibrates in my coat pocket. It's Malik. I pick up.

"Malik, save me!"

"Okay, listen, Ellie, this is an extremely complicated situation. Extremely. I have to…"

A security agent is talking to me at the same time. Hands me a gray plastic bin, orders me to put all my personal effects in it.

I'm slow, I'm holding up the line, he's getting impatient. Tells me to put my phone in the bin, points to the pictograms on the sign.

On the phone, Malik asks, "Ellie? Ellie, are you listening to me?"

"Yes, yes, sorry. I have to take off my shoes, we're going through security. I'll call you back in two seconds."

Text messages between Mila and Samuel
Friday, November 2, 10:26 p.m.

M: I'm shooting a spot with Ellie at your place tomorrow . . .
Will you be there?

S: Don't think so. Why?

M: We're going to be trying on a lot of clothes, it's boring,
you could come and help me undress.

S: What? In front of my girlfriend?

M: Well no, we could play hide and seek. She doesn't need
to know.

10:38 p.m. Mila Mongeau has sent a photo

S: Mila you're cute, but I'm engaged.

M: Don't care.

S: I do, I'm not that kind of guy, sorry.

M: Lol ;)

10:42 p.m. Mila Mongeau has sent a photo

M: I have plenty more if you want. I think of you often.

43

"Okay, sorry, I'm listening! I'm so relieved to talk to you, Malik, you have no idea."

I sit down in the first spot I can find at the boarding gate. Malik always has a solution. He's the best.

"What should we do about this?" I say, full of hope.

"Well, Ellie, the situation is…before anything else, I must tell you that Banana Apparel has withdrawn from the New Year's Festival project. Their VP called me this morning from her skiing holiday, and I can tell you that she is far from happy about this turn of events. Frankly, she would have preferred that you air your dirty laundry elsewhere instead of in a public place —"

"Yes, but it wasn't my idea!"

"According to the contract they signed, you can keep the advance payment, but that will be the only one. The clothes, too. They're yours, but they ask you not to wear them in photos and not to post anything related to them on your pages."

I take in this news.

"But we're already at the airport, our flight leaves in an hour. What do…what can…?"

"Nothing is stopping you from leaving! Take a vacation! Listen, Élisabeth, I also have to tell you that this whole situation puts me in an odd position. Mila is my client, too... Under the circumstances, I... I have no choice but to end our collaboration, at least temporarily. You know this is not a matter of the agency taking sides, but simply put, Mila comes across better in this whole debacle, so under the circumstances... You understand how it is."

"Oh! Oh... okay."

"I have nonetheless contacted a public relations firm. They're very good, they'll help you. I'll give you their number, do you have a pen? No, you know what? I'll text it to you. Then who knows, when the dust settles, maybe we consider collaborating again, eh?"

"Well, yes, or, no, I..."

Through the big windows of the terminal, I see a plane move slowly down the tarmac in the distance. It rolls, turns, reaches the take-off runway, comes to a standstill.

"Off you go, sweetie. Someone from the agency will write you this week to close your files. Be strong and good luck! Hugs to Sam!"

I hold my breath. The plane speeds up, its large wings spread against the wind. It leaves the ground and flies away, disappears in the gray sky.

CELEBRITY WORLD

The Élisabeth Bourdon-Marois Affair: Under pressure from certain internet users, Karma speaks out

In a statement posted on its Facebook page, the Karma Company said that in light of the information available, it "has suspended its partnership with Quinoa Forever for the moment." The company made a point of saying, however, that it is committed to listening and re-evaluating the situation if . . .

Twins Emma & Juju share their experience with Élisabeth Bourdon-Marois

In a series of posts on their Instagram account, the twins Emma and Juliette Stanford, well known for their reality show *The Life of Twins*, shared an anecdote that, according to them, illustrates the temperament Ellie can sometimes have in private. The incident is said to have occurred at the Anti-Bullying Gala, when Ellie purportedly led the twins to believe that her partner, singer Samuel Vanasse, was on site while he . . .

The Élisabeth Bourdon-Marois Affair: Ellie and her agency break ties

On its Instagram page, the B-COZ agency, which has been representing the influencer, announced this morning that it has broken off its relationship with Bourdon-Marois by mutual agreement, on the heels of Mila Mongeau's video this morning, in which she sheds light on her tumultuous relationship with . . .

44

Taking a seat at the edge of the gate area near the concourse, I wait nervously for Sam to return. He went to find something to eat. I drink a very ordinary twelve-dollar coffee and watch our boarding gate. I'm exhausted, tense, overwhelmed. I watch the time on my phone. I've had three missed calls — three calls from my mother. No thanks. I have no desire to talk to her at this moment. She has the compassion of a rock.

In the distance, I see Sam returning, valiantly running down the moving sidewalks as easily as if he were flying.

He makes his way to me, chewing his bagel with cream cheese.

"It's all good. We're sorted. I'm sending the screenshots to a guy who will leak them on Reddit. That's where my contact from *Narcisse* will get them. It's cleaner that way. Thomas promised to try to publish his article within the hour. We'll do the stories in Toronto. We need to start thinking about what to say."

"Okay."

"Imagine if this gave other people courage to speak out. That would be cool! I'll bet there are a ton of juicy stories to dig up about Mila."

"Yeah...well, that's not really necessary, either. She has the right to sleep with whoever she wants. You should understand that better than anyone."

"Stop feeling bad, Ellie. This is no longer the time to play fair. We'll do what we have to do, that's all."

I suspect he's right. The coffee is giving me a headache. I'm dehydrated. Sam scrolls through his conversation with Mila, takes screenshots.

I put myself in her place. If a guy I trusted published our intimate exchanges, I can't imagine how that would make me feel...

"You're not using the photos, are you?"

"No, no. I'm going to hide them."

"And you realize that after this people will never look at you the same way again, right? What if she leaks other messages out of revenge?"

"Maybe, but I would rather look like a player than..."

"Than what?"

He doesn't answer. He's on a mission. His eyes are glued to his phone, he hides the sexy selfies behind big black rectangles. I look around to make sure no one is watching or listening to us. I'm thirsty, and I'm starting to feel a bit sick.

"Shouldn't I talk to the public relations team first?" I say nervously.

He shakes his head, types his email, starts to attach the screen grabs. Between two sips of overpriced coffee, I feel pressure building in my chest — a feeling, a little voice.

My little voice. I hear her! Maybe we've had a few communication problems lately, but right now she is speaking clearly, she is talking to me in all caps.

I don't know whether it's the caffeine rush or the voice of reason, but she's saying, WHAT THE HELL, ELLIE? DON'T DO IT!

Oh, my God, she's right.

I quickly put my hand in front of Sam's phone screen.

"Don't send anything!"

"Stop, you're not serious..."

"Very serious. Don't."

I take his phone out of his hand. I'm afraid he's going to press Send.

"Wait, we have no choice!" he says, outraged.

"Don't count on those public relations pencil pushers to help us. You don't understand —"

"I understand what you want to do, Sam. You want to show that there's a big gap between what Mila says and what she does. I get it. But that's not what people are going to remember. I'm not going to expose her, not with private messages. Can you imagine the abuse she'll get? Wall-to-wall slut shaming! I won't be part of that. It's enough. We've screwed up enough. All three of us."

"Are you defending her after all this?"

"Yes. Yes, I am, even if I'm furious at her, and upset. Even if I blame her. Yes. We do this over my dead body."

He opens his mouth but says nothing.

I need a bottle of water — very expensive water, but YOLO. I get up to go and buy one.

"So what do we do now?" he asks desperately. "Give up? Go home? You're not serious!"

"I don't know. Let me think about it."

For a moment, I set aside Project Hydration. I look out at the tarmac, the planes, looking for a solution in the tons of carbon fiber, aluminum, all the aerospace genius displayed in front of us.

"I'm going to talk to the public relations firm. I'm going to call them."

Sam covers his face with his hand, closes his eyes. He's hunched over, sad.

I take out my cell. I have no intention of calling anyone. I open my apps, deactivate my accounts one by one. Instagram, YouTube, Facebook, TikTok, LinkedIn, Snapchat... I close them all. Wherever I exist, I erase myself, make myself disappear.

It makes me dizzy. I am only here and nowhere else. Just me, just here, just now.

"What about if we do nothing?" I suggest, exhilarated. "If we go on vacation without the contract, without the networks. Just the two of us?"

**Top 10 YouTubers
CAN/FR**

1. Jordanne Jacques – 812,000 followers
2. Tellement Cloé – 764,000 followers
3. Mila Mongeau – 507,000 followers
4. Cath Bonenfant – 504,000 followers
5. Emma & Juju – 498,000 followers
6. Approved by Gwen – 431,000 followers
7. Sophie Chen – 347,000 followers
8. Maëla Djeb – 169,000 followers
9. Zoé around the World – 149,000 followers
10. Léa Mondoux – 111,000 followers

45

Behind the counter, airline staff make the pre-boarding call.

Sam gets up, angry. He paces the floor. I follow him with our bags. My coffee is cold.

He leans against a glass panel.

"You've deactivated your accounts!" he says in dismay. "Wait a minute here. No, Ellie, you can't do that! We have to fight. It's like confessing that you're guilty! Do you understand what you're about to give up?"

"But...it looks like there's nothing to save."

"Seems to me we should have talked about this first!"

"Why? What does it change?"

"Everything!"

He's furious. I gesture for him to calm down, to lower his voice.

"Sam," I add. "I'm taking a break. After this we'll see...maybe I'll come back, maybe this is the best thing that could happen to me. Okay, I'm exaggerating, but...you know what I mean. Like, for a while now I've been wondering whether I might like to stop. Do something else. Clearly it's not making me happy! I don't like the person that I've become."

"But I do! I do like that. I don't want to stop. This is my whole life — the concerts, being out in the world, having big projects like this. I don't want to stop, ever. You can't just stop without telling me. You can't dump our projects in the trash like that!"

The airline employee invites passengers sitting in rows eighteen to thirty-two to make their way to the departure gate.

"But nothing is stopping you from continuing!" I say. "You're not the one who's just been dumped by your agent!"

"Yes, but we can't have that life together."

"We don't know that. We'll see."

"No, you know that at some point things will move quickly...if we don't deal with this immediately... it's over."

"Well...maybe. Let's just —"

"I can't. It's not just your career we're talking about here."

"We have tickets to New Zealand! Just come and —"

"No." He shakes his head. Takes a deep breath, looks at me with a smile that's as sad as the rain.

I watch him in silence, unable to do whatever it might take to change things.

He steps forward, kisses me on the forehead.

"Good luck, my bunny."

"Wait...what?"

The gate agent announces that all remaining passengers are now invited to board.

We look at each other, each of us on different sides of the world.

"But," I whisper, "I thought you loved me."

"I do love you. That has nothing to do with it."

He takes his backpack, gives me a little wave with his hand. He is so sad. So am I. I watch him go. The long corridor, his back, his big solid shoulders, his confident walk. He walks to the exit.

The corridor is long, and it takes forever before he's out of sight.

I watch him fade, become more and more blurry, until he's just a silhouette among all the others. Until he becomes the others. A stranger.

Sam is gone. Sam is gone. I keep repeating it over and over as if it will help make it real, help me to understand.

I hesitate. Do I fall apart right here right now, or

do I go fall apart somewhere else?

I glance at the counter, where the agents are scanning the boarding passes of the last few passengers in line.

I want to, but I don't. I'm afraid of being miserable, but at the same time, no place is more attractive right now than the other side of the world. Enjoy my freedom. Feel giddy.

Okay, I'm going. I'm going to do it. My heart is racing, it's beating to encourage me, to push me forward. I'm going by myself, I can't believe it!

I get in line, get out my passport, my boarding pass. I'm leaving. I can't believe that I am this girl, that I could be so bold.

46

In line to board the plane, my phone vibrates. I think of Dave. Agh, I am pathetic. I have to stop, I'll make it quick.

I take out my phone, look at the screen. It's Alice.

Ah...okay, good. I won't say no to a little tough love, or even maybe a little bit of comfort, encouragement, a phone hug.

I swipe my finger on the green button and get emotional just at the thought of talking to her.

"Hiiii," I say in a little voice. "I'm not doing so good. What about you?"

"Ellie, you're not on the plane yet? Papa is dead."

And I fall apart right here, right now.

PAPA

I only kept the ugly memories — at least mostly. A collection of pain. I'm sorry.

But the photos remind me that I was your baby. That you held me in your arms, fed me, held me tightly against you. That I was your daughter. That you taught me how to ride a bike, walked me to school. That you supported me, watched me grow up. These pictures remind me that you were my father.

As for your love, I only have one translucent, evaporated memory.

I would like him to come back to me one day, this father that you were. Our stories of tenderness, of complicity, of warmth. Do our memories exist somewhere?

I promise to look for them. To wait for them.

But if they don't come, if I can't find them, maybe I need to learn to live without them. Give up all hope of a better past.

1

I'm driving a small moving truck. By myself. Just like that. I mean, it's not nothing. I park in front of the cottage beside Opale's clunker. I gather up my coffee cups, my greasy garbage, all the paper napkins, the ketchup packets. I throw them in a big brown paper bag, get out of the vehicle, stretch my legs and unfreeze my bum, which feels permanently squashed, like two pancakes.

It has been a long trip.

I taste the freshness of the wind, the sound of the snow geese. I've come home. My home. I climb the steps, go into the cottage. The smell. The light.

I could stand here for a long time, enjoying the moment — except for the distraction of seeing my sister in her panties.

"Alice! I'm really tired of seeing your bottom!"

She turns around with a beer in her hand.

"S'up, homie!"

"Weren't you coming tomorrow?"

Opale appears in my field of vision. She bends down to mop up a big puddle of beer with a tea towel.

"Surprise! We're here — and we brought the karaoke machine!"

"Noooo, please..."

I look at them and smile. They look great. I love seeing them together. They wanted me to move into Opale's old bedroom at the apartment, but for now I intend to spend most of my time here. Move my things into the cottage. My father left it to Alice and me.

Opale finishes wiping up.

"After we got all your boxes out of your ex's place, we thought you'd need help unpacking. We just drove faster than you. It wasn't hard. You drive like a turtle."

"Hey, I was driving a heavy vehicle."

"A biggish van..."

"It's a little truck! Have some respect."

"I bow down."

"Good, okay, you're very nice, but if you want to help, try to get your *girlfriend* here to put on some pants."

"They're in the dryer, and you're getting a bit boring with that girlfriend thing. It's getting to be old news."

"You're old news! Don't you get it? You're officially in a relationship!"

"You're an idiot."

"No, you love me. At least as much as your *girlfriend*."

"Jesus."

∞

Once the truck is unloaded, I sit on the balcony overlooking the river. Roll myself up in a quilt, sit in a lounge chair. I am never going to get up again. Ever.

I watch the tide go down, the wild geese heading north. It's the season for them, and they stretch out as far as the eye can see. In the clouds. In the furrows, like little dots. It's beautiful.

I'm still sad sometimes, but it doesn't scare me as much as it used to. I haven't been doing much of anything lately. I often watch the same movies, often eat the same thing, often listen to the same music. I go to bed early.

It was hard at first, but I'm getting used to it. I'm waiting...waiting for things to make sense.

Alice and Opale come out to join me. They each sit in a lawn chair. We don't talk, we listen to the geese chattering and look out at the horizon. Two weeks ago, we spread my father's ashes out in the forest, on the shore, his favorite hunting spot. I imagine that he is still here with us, that he's watching over us.

I don't know what has come over me. I'm suddenly feeling philosophical.

"It's crazy," I say, "to think that before, I just had one sister, and now I'm going to have four."

"Three," Alice corrects. "Me and the twins, that's three."

"No, I count Opale, too. Four sisters. It's nice."

I give Opale a big smile and she bursts out laughing.

"Wow, Ellie! You are such a mushball!"

"Hey, you're not being nice."

I'm a little offended, but I'm laughing anyway.

"I'm kidding," she says. "Except, if you're my sister, that means that I can't sleep with my sister's sister. It would be like incest —"

"Whoa! Okay, cut it out! That'll teach me to express my feelings."

Alice starts talking to Opale about me as if I'm not even there.

"She is a mushball, I warn you. This morning she

357

posted a photo of a little tuft of grass between two small patches of melted snow."

"But it was beautiful," I say loudly, waving my hands. "It's life resuming its course, triumphing over winter. You have no soul!"

Opale keeps talking to Alice.

"Your sister has lost her chops since she started just having a private account. How many followers already, Ellie?"

"Eighteen, but I think I'm going to unfriend you two soon. So that would make sixteen."

"You could have way more. It's not a crime, you know."

"Yes, but not right away. I'm not ready."

Opale takes a pack of gum out of her pocket, takes a piece.

"Okay, look, I am also going to express my feelings. Are you ready?" She clears her throat. "What you're doing is cool. I'm impressed. I never thought you would be able to take a step back or be more chill about food. It's beautiful to see you trying to learn to love your body. I admire you."

It's her turn to give me a big smile. I'm touched, but I don't let it show.

"No, I am not learning to love my body. I am learning to be okay with the fact that I don't love my body. It's not the same thing."

"Big difference."

"Yes! You're just jealous because I'm speeding down the highway of personal growth, and you're not. As proof, I think that I understood something important yesterday."

"What?"

"...I don't need to get back into my costume. I am not Beyoncé."

"Shocking."

"Wait," says Alice. "*Lemonade*? That wasn't you?"

Alice and Opale burst out laughing, and I try to explain.

"What I mean is..."

"No, it's good for you to clarify, because I get the two of you mixed up all the time..."

They're kidding around.

"Okay, forget it," I say, rolling my eyes. "You are so annoying!"

Slightly below the horizon line, between the clear gray of the river and the white clouds, the sky is turning pinky orange. It's on fire, showing off.

"Oh, Ellie," Alice says, "don't sulk. We're listening. Go on...!"

"What I mean is that I'm working to remember that... I am not my body."

The wind rises. It smells of manure, woodsmoke and tall grass. The sky is all pink. It is bewitching.

I shrug my shoulders.

"I am not my body."

#PARTNERS

A huge thanks to:

OLIVIER, thanks for everything! Thanks for having been a part of this journey. You are awesome.

JOËLLE, the best. I love you, I couldn't have hoped for anyone better to guide this project. I hope our collaboration will continue forever.

CHRISTINE, for the good advice, the critical eye and care. Thank you for understanding me so well.

MARTIN, for your unfailing support, your kindness and your trust.

CATHERINE, for the difficult but rewarding discussions.

MARIE, my favorite bookseller, for your enthusiasm and little words of encouragement that make all the difference.

DANIELLE FICHAUD, I realize that I write the way I play. And you're the one who taught me how to play. Thank you for that, from the bottom of my heart.

The entire team at LA BAGNOLE, with special thanks to SARAH, CLÉMENCE, MARIKE and GENEVIÈVE.

Finally, the writing of this novel has been made possible thanks to the unwavering support of my coffee machine — you're the best, baby — and my family of love — Anne-Marie, Béa, Pom, Paul and Madeleine. Thank you for being there.

LAURENCE BEAUDOIN-MASSE spent her adolescence envying the girls on the volleyball team and living great love stories...in her head. She can truthfully say that she has never been asked to slow dance in her life. As an adult, she is fascinated by influencers, whom she likes to gently mock. She has written two novels: *Suck It In and Smile* (originally published as *Rentrer son ventre et sourire*) and its sequel, *Say Yes and Keep Smiling*. She is a concept editor for CBC/Radio-Canada. She lives in Montreal, Quebec.

SHELLEY TANAKA is an award-winning author, translator and editor who has written and translated more than thirty books. She teaches at Vermont College of Fine Arts. Shelley lives in Kingston, Ontario.